The Precipice

By

Billy Harding

The *1st* Will Hardley Novel

4

Well here it is.

My debut Novel.

So, I dedicate this story firstly:

To my very own '3 J's' who inspired me as this idea of one evening entirely set in a Gay Pub sat in my mind for a number of years as I served customers their coffee at my normal job. To my own *Son of a Tutu*, the very first Drag Queen I ever saw perform in person, you inspire me with your humour, kindness, uniqueness, and wit every day. You absolutely deserve to be in this story, and I wouldn't have it any other way.

Secondly:

This is also part-dedicated to every single person I ever ran this idea by & they told me they really liked the sound of it. Your messages of telling me to not give up were just the motivation I needed. Thank you.

& Thirdly:

I dedicate this to any 'LGBT+ Safe Space Bar or Pub' not situated in a major City but off the beaten track in Towns & Villages' in all four Regions of the UK. Your very existence is so important to helping young people find their identities whilst nurturing them or even better yet, helping others who wait later in their lives to accept themselves with confidence, I thank you for that.

Billy Harding © 2020

One

Saturday, October 15th, 2016.

Basildon.

Essex.

8:10 PM...

Will Hardley was tired, no not tired. He was drained yet not in the pleasurable way he normally liked. He needed a proper man to do that which had been sorely lacking recently. It's Saturday night and he quite frankly needed a much-required energy boost, only a few short years ago he would have been raring to go for a night out on the town.

Now he was a twenty five year old with a somewhat depleted amount of energy on his way out to the edge of Essex with three mates to a place he hadn't set foot in about eleven months to the day since he last checked his tagged stuff on Social Media.

'I used to look forward these kinds of things. Now I am pretty muted' Will thought to himself on the train as it rolled to a stop in Basildon. "So, Johnny" Will began "we gotta meet Josh here then he'll drive us the rest of the way, come on" springing up from the train seat to disembark with some added gusto still trying to get his reserves to spike once more. Johnny Michaels followed Will off the train and out of Basildon Station "how long will we have to wait for Josh do you think?" Johnny asked "well we are doing well for time since we have to be there after 9 for Tutu who will be on stage after or around 10:30 so he should be here in the next few minutes" Will replied checking his phone for any WhatsApp Messages from their designated driver and mate Josh

Sullivan. Will had known both Johnny and Josh for good stretches of time, Josh since the inception of the 2010's then Johnny since 2012 before the Olympics had descended on London like a plague, sure tourism went through the roof but everything else went to shit in the process. Great for the UK's history books, not so great for anyone working in or around the City then having to commute out of it on a daily basis. Will had stumbled upon Josh and Johnny through the so called 'dating' but well known 'hook-up' app that was Grindr with varying degrees of success. Josh had remained firmly in the Friendship Zone while Johnny dabbled in the Friends with Benefits concept much to Wills delighted agreement; they all had needs attending to after all. Now four and six years later here they still were in Wills Life for the right reasons. Checking his phone, Will saw the WhatsApp Message he had been hoping for:

On the way. Be ready for pick up at the back. 20:14

"Aha!" Will exclaimed which got Johnny's attention "Josh is en route to the station in his car, won't be long" pocketing his mobile, "good cause its getting chilly" Johnny said rubbing his arms quickly "so who else is coming tonight again?" Johnny enquired. "Hmm it's kind of interesting as its Josh's ex-boyfriend Joe but their now in the friend's zone but they both still have this...well this *thing* going on..." Will didn't finish the answer because he didn't know all the facts of the situation either, but Johnny could guess "when you say *thing* do you mean they're still shagging?" Johnny asked quiet but forwardly causing Will to snap his head round in surprise "well, well Johnny Michaels *meow*" Will teased his best mate which elicited a tut plus a folding of the arms from Johnny "what on earth made you think it was that anyway you *naughty boy*?" Will teased further with a devilish look along with a nudge but Johnny didn't rise to it "I was just saying that's all since we know Josh likes them a bit younger" Johnny responded having found some obscure object off in the distance to occupy his interest rather conveniently. "Well you have a point about that I guess" Will agreed partially with Johnny's assessment.

Having come out then making their way to the back of the station they were waiting for Josh to turn up in his car in the increasingly chilly October weather. Where they were heading would only be colder still. Then going just, a touch too fast Josh arrived to pick them up with the passenger seat window already down, "hey Gay Boys! Ready for a night out" Josh hollered from the driver's seat "Will, can we expect you to be paralytic again like last time in Gran Canaria..." Josh sniggered as Will took the front seat while Johnny took the rear seat laughing softly at the joke. "At least I'm a funny paralytic and not a useless piece of meat that snores on holiday" Will fired back to more laughter from Josh. "*Touché*" Josh retorted as he set off back on the road before the boys had even got their seatbelts locked in place "always in a hurry aren't ya *Sullivan*" Will noted as they made their way through Basildon to pick up Josh's exbf/friend/whatever he was. "You know me, not a lot of patience for much these days" Josh kept his eyes on the road for once "So Joe is joining us on our little adventure tonight then?" Will side-eyed Josh from the passenger seat clearly fishing for some juicy gossip to entertain him and Johnny on the journey, Johnny of course correctly didn't add anything extra to the already loaded question. "Yes, he is and not a word or snarky comment out of you *Hardley*" Josh maintained his eyes on the road to Wills very fabricated and over the top horrified face "me! Making suggestive or specific comments, well Josh I thought you knew me better than that" Will finished in a mocking fashion by turning his face to look out the car window but Josh wasn't letting him off that easily while Johnny remained ever so quiet in the back but enraptured by the camaraderie going on in the front, "yes you do make those kind of comments Will so this little Bo Peep act ain't holding up much stock plus your twenty five so the innocent thing really kind of got lost on you when you lost your virginity at sixteen Mr" Josh continued to

Wills genuine shock this time. "Oh, we're using our ages against one another, now are we? Well Mr Josh two can play at that game, how old is Joe, exactly?" Will put on the butter wouldn't melt tone to his voice which got a small laugh from the ever-quiet Johnny but a defiant quietness from Josh.

"Josh... How old is Joe again?"

"Old enough."

"Yes, but how old *exactly*?"

"Not important."

"Oh, I think it is don't you agree Johnny?"

"Why you asking him!"

"I wouldn't mind knowing myself..."

Josh then muffled something, but the boys couldn't make it out. "Could you repeat that pretty please *Joshy*" Will mocked some more in a child's voice, "he's twenty-one ok" Josh finally answered the lingering question to silence from the boys.

"Joe is twenty-one years old then eh? And what is your age as well Josh?"

Josh mumbled another response.

"SPEAK UP Josh, we didn't catch that!" Will egged the situation for all its worth but Josh wasn't budging this time then a response came from an unlikely source, "Josh is thirty-seven" Johnny answered Wills question clearly in the back seat whilst he had found something to look at on his phone in timely manner. Will then cackled like a proud witch whilst Josh turned on Johnny "whose side are you on now backseat driver!", "*what?*" Johnny enquired innocently which made Josh go back to his slightly embarrassed silence. "Oh, I am enjoying this, so Johnny that gives us an age differential of..."

"Sixteen years in total give or take a few months."

"Josh you sly dog, we always knew you liked them young but this one is younger than me and Johnny by four whole years!" Will finished the roasting of his friend with gleeful abandonment; Josh maintained his silence for a few moments as the driving continued through Basildon's streets to the destination of the much-discussed Joe. Will was smug, Johnny was content, and Josh relaxed after his roasting. When they were nearing their final pick up stop Josh decided to resume, "so yeah no more suggestive comments or conversations about me or Joe Will understand. We are mates that's all just working out where we stand with one another" he stated rather bluntly which got Wills full attention once more. "Cor you really don't want us to learn whatever is going on between you two do ya Sullivan" Will threw up his hands in mock surrender "alright message received loud and clear. No mention of your particular situation with your toy boy" Will finished much to the relief of Josh but there was one last little dig, there always was with Will.

"One thing I'm curious about that is bugging me..."

"Whatever it is, don't say it Will"

"I just *have* to get it off my chest Josh"

"You really don't."

 "Oh but I do"

"Ugh, what is it?"

"Does he call you *Daddy*? You know when you two use too..." Will made a suggestive movement that required the use of both of his hands.

Josh came to a set of traffic lights with surprisingly calm precision. He looked at the red light for a moment then slowly but surely turned to face the mischievous Will who had a full faced grin on his whilst Johnny observed the two guys like it was some very convoluted but highly interesting tennis match. "Do you wanna walk to where we are going cause its now coming up to 8:30, we gotta pick up Joe, we still have to get on the dual carriageway and don't get me started on the actual parking at the place. *If* Joe calls me that word, which is very much our business that stays between him and I, wouldn't you say so?" Josh resumed looking at the headlights which were now turning green. Will kept his grin on but his eyes had narrowed "fine, you win. But I'm gonna call you Daddy from now on. Consider it your nickname, plus before you throw a hissy fit again you more than rock the look so take it as compliment if anything else" Will concluded returning his filthy mind and face to the road ahead. "Whatever. Bitch." Josh turned a couple of more streets to finally reach their first destination, Joe Mason. All six foot and three inches of him. They pulled up outside his detached house and he came round the car to take the final back seat next to Johnny, "hey Queens!" Joe exclaimed plugging himself in "we all ready for a night out?" He asked which got two silent responses from Josh and Johnny so Will seized the opportunity and took point on the conversation "oh yes I need an alcoholic beverage my dear. I'm in the mood for beer tonight in fact..." Will stopped when Josh startled chuckling to himself "What now?" Will asked "on the beer, camp little thing like you. Take it all the vodka and cokes you consumed from Gran Can back in May were a little bit too much...", Josh prodded Will who raised his eyebrows defensively but wasn't about to take it lying down "I'll have you know I plan to last tonight not be on my *last legs* after the first hour of being there thank you very much. If there happens to be the odd shot of something going on offer, then..."

"You'll be anyone's?" Josh finished which got raucous laughs out of both Jo and Johnny much to Wills now truly shocked face.

"I am not that easy for one thing you lot" he said in retaliation this time finding something to amuse him out of the car window. "Will" Josh called to him from the driving seat; Will half turned towards him with his eyes narrowed once again "two can play at that game can't they!" Josh laughed out loud along with further ones from Joe and Johnny also as Will gave up properly with his and Josh's so called banter by folding his arms then eyeballing the road ahead for all its worth internally daring it to swallow him, as they made their out of Basildon and onto their final destination.

*

Leaving the flat, industrialized lands of Basildon behind, Josh made his way onto the A127 dual carriageway. They were a motley crew the four of them. Josh the dad, Johnny the quiet, Joe the young and Will the sassy. It makes for an interesting car journey to say the least. They were all heading out because why not, it's Saturday night and there is Life to be lived. *'If we can ever get there in time that is'* Will thought to himself as they sped down the carriageway Josh was one thing if not dominant on the road. "So, gang, can I call us a gang? How about Foursome? What are we all planning from tonight besides alcohol?" Josh let the question hang there in the open, Joe jumped in first "I wanna enjoy my time with you guys obviously, Johnny?" Johnny looked at Joe "well I've actually never been to this place before" Johnny began but was drowned out by gasps from Joe and Josh.

"Seriously" Joe said sparing a quick look from the rear-view mirror at Johnny.

"You're kidding right?" Joe had his hand on his chest which wasn't faked either.

Will then timed in to defend his best mate. "Yep its true I'm afraid he has never been to this place. This is why I think we all need to agree we have a little *homework assignment* for Johnny don't you think boys?" after letting that statement hang in the air all three of the Foursome were hanging on to Wills words wondering where he was going with this, "so Johnny, tonight you have one simple task", "Which is?" Johnny replied "you have to have an *orgy* while you're there. They have a spare room upstairs for them every Saturday." Will deadpanned but Johnny's horrified face wasn't plastered on for long as Josh and Joe both came to his defence quickly.

"Oi Will, stop winding him up!"

"Yeah cut it out. The poor guy nearly shat himself when you said that..."

Will sniggered at his own joke as he turned around to see Johnny giving him a full-on bug eyed look over his glasses. Still smirking he continued "no, no don't worry your precious little head Johnny boy. All you have to do when your there is something extremely easy that all of us have done many a times in our lives so far..." Will paused just to add a little dramatic effect as the car carried on down the A127. Joe was getting impatient with the suspense now "which is what? Come on even I wanna know!" he was practically bouncing up and down in his passenger seat for the answer. Johnny ever the quiet one kept his buy eyed look up but was curious about what it was. "Your official homework assignment Johnny Michaels is when we get to where we are going..." Will continued

"...all you have to do is *watch and observe*" he finished with a fixed but neutral smile. Johnny had no idea what on earth he was even talking about while Josh and Joe both seemed to be realising what Will was referencing.

"Ah Will your on to something there mate."

"Yeah that's actually a good one."

"So yeah there we have it, any ideas about your homework Johnny?" Will asked his best friend, "Not a clue, but I'll do what you ask of me" Johnny answered but he was unsure about what else he could say on the matter. Johnny looked out of the window of the car to ponder what had been set for him to do, he noticed that the landscape had changed somewhat since they had departed Basildon. They were now entering Southend-On-Sea having come off the dual carriageway and just driven past the welcome sign and there it was, the River Thames. Johnny was just able to make out the Thames in the night, all peaceful and still. The world probably around this time is the best time to take it in even though he could barely make out the water itself. It was soothing as he wondered what was expected of him this evening. He still had no idea as he returned his attention back into the car where the activity was, Joe was on his phone answering a text while Josh and Will chatted in the front.

"...All I'm saying is even if I have a few shots tonight I won't be an absolute mess like I was in Gran Can *Josh*" Will was defending himself again but Josh didn't seem to be buying it "look, like you said I've known you six years. I know your tolerance levels plus how much drink you can reasonably handle but I swear if you're sick in my car tonight your cleaning it up Will" Josh laid down the law but Will was already accepting whatever superficial punishment Josh was placing on his shoulders. "At least you know I take responsibility for my actions unlike say your roommate at your house Josh" Will pointed out but Josh was rolling his eyes as he kept driving, "that's an entirely different and unnecessary conversation for another time anyway which has no relevance to all of us on a night out" he finished. "Well you can't say I'm not mindful but we were on holiday so I let my hair down" Will said but Josh chuckled again "what hair Will? You yourself said it's been receding since you were *fifteen* when you started getting questions about it in school" Josh sarcastically made his point as Will side eyed him "poor use of words if you ask me Will since there isn't a lot of hair left for you. Might wanna still think about that hair transplant?" Josh finished his joke but as always Will had an answer for everything, "ok, ok I was just using an age-old expression to make a point which you all know." Will finished the conversation before it became an open can of worms that couldn't be contained. "Anyway gang, we're almost there now thankfully. Sod ever driving from Hornchurch down to Southend it's at least fifty minutes one way from your neck of the woods Johnny and Will. Least in Basildon its only about twenty-five to thirty minutes tops" their designated driver breathed a sigh of relief. He was getting a bit long in the tooth for nights out like this '*one day I will see the back of these journeys driving the lads when their pissed whilst I'm still sober, not that I drink anyway*' Josh mused to himself. Truth be told he did kind of tire of where they were going, with the right people like to tonight it would be fun for some of it, but when he hadn't been with the boys it wasn't all that cracked up to be. Not like it use to be anyway.

"Well since we're almost there I'm getting the first round in lads, so what will be all be having?" Joe asked to the peaked interest of the Foursome.

"Coke for me since I'm the designated driver" Josh called out.

"Corona Extra with lemon for moi", Will was raising his hand in acknowledgement.

"Amaretto and Coke please" Johnny asked.

"Excellent, then I'll have glass of Rose" Joe clapped his hands together eager to signal the night was about to get underway. Josh had slowed down the car a lot since disembarking off the A127 to enter Southend. They were driving down the high street away from the hustle and bustle of crowds out on their own Saturday night adventures to whatever clubs, turning round the corner to go past Southend Central train station, up the road, then a quick right turn across a small bridge above the train tracks to see their final destination awaiting them on the street corner with long row of houses opposite. Josh saw a parking space just up from where they were heading and grabbed it while it was there, even if there were double yellow lines were clearly preventing them from parking there in an official capacity.

"Err do you not see the double yellows your car is blatantly parked on top of Josh?" Will enquired as they got out of the car stretching his legs as he went. "Nah don't worry about it, the traffic wardens are done for the day round here so will be alright for the night, besides, I'll come and check on the car once or twice while we're here anyway. You can leave your coats in the car if you like"

Josh said staring at their destination chucking his coat accordingly back in the vehicle with little regard then shut his door which the other guys followed suit with as well. They all stood as a group taking a quick moment to look at where they would be spending their evening. "Well boys...let's do this shall we?" Will stated then led the way forward to the venue.

Their night had begun at The Precipice.

Two

The Precipice Pub.

Southend-On-Sea.

Essex.

9:10 PM...

The Foursome entered The Precipice Pub, and it was quiet still for all intents and purposes. The lack of people near the bar gave them a clear shot of getting served quickly before the rest of whatever the potential crowd arrived for the night's shenanigans. Will took in the interior, one pool table, and one rather small stage if you could call it that, one long bar then further along with an extended bit that went out the back under a small one-person at a time archway where a few other tables were situated. It wasn't a huge space by any stretch of the imagination, but it was compact for what it was yet served its purpose well for a Gay Bar. For Will it was like greeting an old mate you didn't see that often, but the familiar sights, sounds, smells and atmosphere were a welcoming comfort, nonetheless. '*Yet I never make it a habit to come here often. Why do I do that again?*' Will questioned to himself little realising the boys had given up being led to him and were already getting the drinks in at the bar by a lady with a set of almost frizzy but curly blonde hair and a set of thick rimmed glasses similar to Johnny's with a cocky smile in place. "Sophie Harriett you bitch come n give us a kiss!" Will almost whooped as he jumped half on to the bar to give Sophie kisses on either cheek which she gratefully accepted. "Willy boy, where have ya been young man! You don't visit us often down this way these days" Sophie responded in kind "how's life treating ya? All good I hope?" Sophie asked but she already had one beady eye fixed on the rest of the bar making sure the staff were serving the other patrons as well, she was the bar manager after all and never missed a trick on her watch. "Well you know how it goes Mrs, stay away long enough then the need and want to visit this place is all the more greater" Will replied "how's it been in this place? Not a lots changed I see with the crowd arriving later as per the usual norm down here" Will asked as one of the songs made famous by *Steps* started playing on the sound system, it was of course Chain Reaction. '*Oh, I am definitely back if they are still replaying Steps*' Will couldn't help but be amused by the typical music choices always on repeat in a place like this. "Ah you know how it goes Willy..." Selma began as she got the boys drinks ready "...you cater to what you know and the crowd here are very much use to the same thing since it's not a big 'Community or Scene' if you like down in good ol Southend" Sophie finished as

Joe paid up for the first round then she set off to check the other customers waiting. "Well boys" Will raised his ice-cold Corona Extra with Lemon "here's to our little adventure this evening" he finished and they all clinked their drinks with aplomb. Taking a healthy gulp on the beer felt good for Will as any of the frustrations he had felt for work ebbed away and he also felt the tiredness slightly wear off too, nothing like an instant hit of alcohol to cure your woes from time to time. Taking another look around the pub he noticed that there still wasn't much of a crowd but some small groups all keeping to themselves, then the Hen Party came walking through the door. All twelve of them. "Well this night just took an interesting turn plus we've only just arrived. Lord knows what else is gonna happen now we have actual Hens in our midst ah lads" Josh chuckled as he sipped his coke "are you kidding?" Joe began "this night took a great turn, there's even a couple of lads with these Hens" Joe sipped his wine with a devilish grin plastered fully on his face as he surveyed the Hen Party which Josh took notice of, as did Will also noticing his friends subtle reaction *'that's not a good sign'* Will foreboded. The Party set up shop away from the Foursome which seemed to alleviate Josh's cautiousness as Joe seemed to lose interest for the time being but Will was sure that was going to cause something between the two whatever-they-were, he would however keep an eye on them both no question about it. The pub was now starting to get an influx of people through its double doors as the hour crept closer to ten, some there purely for the booze, some for the pool which was being slowly coveted by a gaggle of rather butch lesbians, some most probably for the upcoming Drag Show. Sophie was in her element with her staff behind the bar like a finely tuned machine not missing a beat with the growing custom. The place would soon be rowdy and ready for anything with the Foursome very much in the thick of it. Will was enjoying the vibe that had taken hold with the boys who had now resorted to a good old-fashioned game of people watching and what their potential stories were for the evening. "What about the lesbians hogging the pool table?" Will threw that question out for the boys as he started on his second Corona of the night, "what about them?" Josh got in first with the response. "Well, their lesbians, their playing a lot of pool..." Will began but couldn't form a good finish for his sentence; Johnny then out of nowhere chimed in "you mean whose girlfriend is who and by playing *lots of pool* you're wondering if their trying to one-woman ups each other so their girlfriend looks better than the others." Johnny finished as he continued enjoying his Amaretto and Coke. All three of the boys had a set look from his rather pointed response; Will had his beer frozen just before entering his mouth which was almost slack jawed of its own accord, Joe's eyebrows seemed to have disappeared into his brown curly hair whilst Josh was staring at one of the windows with a rather confused look permanently fixed to his face trying to form words of any kind. Blinking hard once Will was able to finally find some words "that was...rather specific Johnny. Where on earth did you figure that all out?", "Well you did say watch and observe"

Johnny answered whilst trying to see if he had any imaginary dust on his glasses, but Joe and Josh were both ready to counter this.

"Yeah but there's watching then there's *watching* Queen..." Joe finished the last of his Rose.

"Exactly, talk about really bloody *specific* Johnny..." Josh tucked into his coke.

Johnny however tried to use the innocent act again "well you did give me the homework assignment" Johnny tried but the two on-off lovers were not having it as they both began speaking at the same time. Seeing his opportunity to duck out and get the next round in rather than add his own opinion into the mix for once Will made his excuses to get back to the bar leaving Joe and Josh to try and work out for themselves how Johnny's mind operated *'that's gonna be one amusing conversation for them all'* Will sniggered to himself as he waited at the now much busier bar. Sophie was on it however without even breaking a sweat going from one patron to the other; she waved absently at Will acknowledging him as he caught her eye, but he was in the queue happy to wait. Will caught the double doors of the pub opening again out of the corner of his eye, turning that's when he saw the duo entering. Mike Harkness and Carl Simpson. '*Oh great, of course these two would be here when Tutu would be performing tonight. I should have mentally prepared myself more*' Will begrudgingly thought as he continued to wait to be served. Mike and Carl were stalwarts of the Southend Scene, no correction they were more like *veterans* of the Scene. Both were about an easy decade older than Will, closer to Josh's age give or a take a year or two's difference even if they weren't close friends but more like casual acquaintances. They weren't only respected at the pub they were for better or worse had an established built in status with the owner and the local Community; they couldn't put a foot wrong if they even tried to go out of their way to offend the Southend Scene. It didn't make them bad people bear in mind, but it did make them very much an untouchable force or element.

Will had always gotten along with both of them equally but he had learnt very early on to be friendly to them when first introduced rather than being an enemy or even worse a frenemy, he wasn't stupid when it came to so-called status when dealing with such a small group of gays because down here it could quite quickly become every person for themselves if you were placed on the outside and sometimes it had happened, just not to him luckily. It was one of the reasons why Will didn't really visit often but he knew he would be welcomed with open arms by maintaining good relations because of those sporadically timed visits. *'Be nice rather than an out and out bitch'* Will had memorised when he first met the self-entitled duo some years prior. He waved at them which caught Mike's attention, but Carl hadn't noticed, not the cute, dark haired and delightfully tall Carl who sat in the tallness spectrum right between Joe and Johnny's heights which did wonders for Will's dirty mind. *'Oh god why do they have to be here tonight'* Will thought glumly turning back as one of Sophie's bar staff finally had time to serve him, he ordered the same round again while Mike and Carl were being helloed and welcomed by the loyal crowd who were between them much to Will's relief for the moment. He would deal with them when it came to that later, for now he was grateful for the increased crowd. Turning his head, the other way to intentionally distract himself as he waited for his drinks to arrive Will saw the Hen Party getting down to business with gusto. What must have been their second or third round of shots for the night *'the first of many'* Will mused internally at how drunk each member of the twelve person group would become then Will nearly dropped his fresh Corona he had just picked up when he did a double take at one of the two lads Joe had spotted in then Hen Party earlier on. "Holy. Shit!" Will muttered aloud *'what the fuck is Ryan Tate doing with them?'* reverting to his thoughts. With a shocked face he put down his beverage and stared at the rest of the new round of drinks he had just finished paying for like they had all the answers. *'Not one but two guys I have had serious flirtations within the past are here tonight, why does this always happen to me!'* Will continued staring at the drinks. This night really had taken a funny but unexpected turn thus far.

And the Foursome had only been there just over an hour.

*

10:13 PM...

Joe, Johnny, and Josh were still debating how Johnny's mind worked in such specificity when Will finally returned with the next round, taking a break from it they all took a much-needed swig each out of their beverages. Johnny noticed how Will wasn't drinking his beer with as much enthusiasm as before. "What's up with you?" Johnny asked which seemed to snap Will out of his daze. "Oh err; well those two have arrived if you guys hadn't noticed..." Will indicated with his drink to Mike and Carl who still seemed to have a small crowd still waiting to greet them. All three-quarters of the Foursome understood all too well, however.

"Aha, their Majesties gracing their subjects with their presence" Josh sarcastically mocked.

"Yep they do love to maintain their presence in their dominion" Joe stated as a matter of fact.

"Their nice, enough aren't they?" Johnny began but then stopped as three pairs of eyes were once again back on to his introverted self, this wasn't a debate or discussion, it was pure facts. "Yeah ok" Will began "but they do seem to live for their crowd since they know no one questions them here ever because they do a lot for this place" he continued "but who are they really once they walk out those doors to go home or back to their jobs? I can imagine not having the attention on them a bit definitely gets to them, right under their skin in fact if I was betting man" Will finished with a big refreshing swig of alcohol. Two Coronas in and he wasn't really feeling their full effect yet, maybe a shot was in order. "You may well be right about that but imagine going up against them?" Josh countered Wills argument "This place would turn on you faster than any young 'Twink' that is new to the Southend Scene and out on the pull with all their rampant sexual energy. Then you wouldn't be welcomed anymore, and you know it" Josh concluded satisfyingly as Will nodded to his friends obvious guarded warning, "yes, yes your quite right as well Sullivan hence why I made nice rather than made nasty. But I mean, look at those two..." Will stopped as the Foursome observed as Mike and Carl finish their necessary hellos. "It's like their deities or something. We would never get that kind of welcome here in a *million years* easily".

"Would you really want that kind of attention as nice as they convey themselves to the crowd though Will?" Josh asked honestly and Will actually didn't have a response for him. "That's what I thought" Josh smirked a little. Joe was starting to get restless as the camp music stopped for a second to be replaced by an announcement, *"oioi you rowdy lot!"* Sophie's voiced came through crisp and clear on the sound system to whoops and catcalls from the crowd milling around the small space, even the butch lesbians stopped playing their intense game of pool to listen in for a moment. *"Now I have all you pissheads attention for a hot second, don't worry you'll get more bladdered as the night wears on I promise you that with our affordable prices. Sod London..."* Sophie got a few cheers for that *"...but you have all got approximately fifteen minutes, yep that's right fifteen minutes of shots, quick fag breaks outside and the odd slash in the bog before we get ready for a good Drag Show by the return of the one and only Son of a Tutu tonight for one night only at The Precipice, see you at the bar bitches!"* Sophie finished her crowd pleasing announcement as the music took over again, this time it was classic *Kylie Minogue* Spinning Around which got the Hen Party doubly excited, the butch lesbians groaning, Mike and Carl finally free from their fan base started swaying to the lyrics while the Foursome took in the sights going

on around them all at once. "Anyone wanna join me for a quick smoke before this place gets even more camper when Tutu comes on?" Joe enquired. Johnny and Josh made themselves busy by both offering to get the third round in at the same time then decided they would just help each other at the bar equally which conveniently left only Will who just shrugged in acknowledgement. "C'mon Joe my dear *Queen*, I'll keep you company even if I don't smoke" Will nudged Joe who flashed a cheeky appreciative grin, the two boys weaved their way through the now pretty full gay bar and exited out of the double doors into the chilly Essex air once more.

*

10:25 PM...

Things were always calmer when you viewed the pub from the outside in, especially when it came to a place like this. '*I bet the neighbours love to people watch this place as much as I do, almost religiously too*' Will surmised as the dedicated smokers including Joe enjoyed their respective nicotine fixes despite the cold October weather. Truthfully Will was little grateful to be alone with Joe so he could pick his brain about what was really going on with him and Josh, so he did what he always did, dived in headfirst. "So spill the beans Joe Mason..." he went straight for it "...what's going on with you and my mate Josh otherwise known as *Daddy*" Will kept his tone playful but pointed for Joe to pick up he wanted to get to the gossip right away. Joe was halfway through his cigarette took another drag inhaling the smoke with a thoughtful look about him, Will was doing all he could to not jump up and down on the spot with impatience. "Ok..." Joe finally started "so yes Josh and I *were* dating. Now we aren't" Joe finished with a simple shrug continuing with his ciggie. Will wasn't buying it however "ah Joe it's never as simple as that mate. I met you through him when he introduced you to me as his boyfriend plus you too were pretty smitten together at the time. What changed? Or better yet *who* changed?" Will just went in with the loaded question which got a more surprised reaction back from Joe who promptly lit a second cigarette in quick succession. "Well you know how it goes Will. People change over time as they say..." Joe trailed off because this time he wasn't intentionally looking Will in the eye, *'aha got you now Mr'* Will heard the metaphorical light bulb go off. Joe was avoiding eye contact intentionally which could only mean that Joe was guilty or feeling guilty about something to do with his complicated liaisons with Josh. "Listen Joe, I've known Josh a long time ok. Yeah sure me and him may have talked but not acted on about blurring the lines once upon a blue moon between friendship and fun but look at us now? A highly dysfunctional friendship that shouldn't really work yet it does. I mean he is thirteen years my senior, we bicker like siblings who don't get along and I wouldn't have it any other way between us so our friendship is more than solid" Will retracted his gossipy ways which made Joe relax as he got through his second cigarette far too quickly but it seemed to bring him back onside. What seemed like a small eternity between the two guys, Will finally got a response "I do care about him Will, know that. But things have gone on between me and Josh that are ours to burden" Joe began to conclude "But whatever we have right now? I'm ok with that for the time being, sex or no sex." Joe finished his sentence by looking at the road which meant Will had an answer, just not the complete one he wanted. He could still feel there was an underlying issue at play with Joe and Josh, it may not have come across the way he wanted but Will wanted to help Josh any way he could to repair whatever had happened between them or try as best as he could anyway. Friendships mattered in this day and age regardless of sexuality.

Checking his phone quickly he then noticed the time in the corner of the screen.

"Joe it's well gone 10:30..."

"Yeah and?"

"Shouldn't Tutu already be on the stage right now doing her first number?"

"Oh, that's a good point actually..."

"WILL!" a booming voice came out of nowhere.

Joe and Wills heads snapped round to the right in unison from where the sound of the voice came from. There standing about ten feet away from them was a man in plain ordinary clothes with a cap on his head who came striding over to the two guys with a confidence or better yet swagger that Will knew all too well. With his practically glowing smooth ebony skin, infectious smile, hands on hips, Will knew this person. He had after all seen him as a she on many Cabaret Stages roasting members of the general public for all they were worth with his massively gorgeous signature headdresses. Now he was in Southend of all places, out of his costume, civilian clothes in place and there was only one thing Will could do there and then.

"TUTU!" he exclaimed opening his arms for a hug to tonight's entertainment act.

'But you're not even in full Drag and you're supposed to be on stage right now!' Will thought alarmingly.

Three

The Smoking Area.

10:35 PM...

"Tutu, the stage is inside there and you're out here being distinctly unfeminine or singing..." Will stated more than asked as he released the Drag Queen from his welcoming hug with another quick look at his boyish attire. Tutu however gave a loud chuckle flashing a full set of overly white teeth *'someone has had them done well'* Will noted of the seasoned Queen who was still smirking at him.

"Willy, Willy you know how it goes in the world of Cabaret performers who travel regularly for a living my dear super fans..." Tutu began who acknowledged Joe as well "...a Queen is never late, the royal subjects simply wait for them" the Drag Queen finished with a small flourish of their hands to strike a camp pose whilst still dressed as man but Will wasn't buying it for a second. Smirking as well he put his hands on his hips in a mock fashion and eyeballed the performer he admired so much then went in for the kill "your train was delayed so you texted ahead to let them know you're gonna be late I'm taking it" he finished with raised eyebrows whilst Joe stood beside him and suppressed a giggle with his hand at the Drag Queens over the top reaction to such a bold claim. Putting one of his hands over his heart area in still overly campy shock Tutu was milking the innocence act for all its worth "Will! I must say that I am disappointed..." Tutu stopped when Will crossed his arms over his chest with some narrowed eyes that could call out anyone on their lying game, surrendering after this Tutu came out with the real truth in defeat. "You are one of the good ones my dearest Will" the Queen let his arms fall to his sides with another small laugh "your quite right, the train which is normally such a reliable service had this performer just a *touch* on the late side so I thought ahead in earnest like any good performer would do" they finished which satisfied Will ten-fold. "You see Tutu in Drag I would never even dare attempt to cross you cause number one you're a formidable force when you have your armour on" Will spoke of the Queen in full admiration this time which got him a proper smile of acknowledgment in kind "number two also. This place is lucky they can even book a talent like you any day since you are in demand in good ol' London town and beyond" Will finished with a sweep of his arms to the train tracks just underneath the bridge across the road. Taking a compliment like this in their stride Tutu put a reassuring yet comforting arm around his fan "Ah Willy boy you really do know to compliment a lady don't you" Tutu teased him as he gave his shoulder a good squeeze, "so tell me how is the crowd in there? I'm not playing to a dead pub am I..." the Queen had a little look in through the double doors briefly but seemed to accept the size of the audience at first glance. Joe was ready to chip in this time "oh don't you worry my dear Queen..." Joe chimed in just when was needed which got Tutu's full attention "...that crowd is gonna eat you up or should I say your gonna devour them" he finished with his signature devilish grin which got a loud laugh in response from Tutu, "ah I like this one Willy, he one of your latest squeezes?" Tutu winked as Wills jaw dropped in total surprise at the Queens unexpected insinuation which had Joe guffawing with no attempt to hide it this instance. "First of all..." Will turned looking at Joe as Tutu took his arm away from him "why are you laughing? You would be lucky to have all of this" Will indicated himself head to toe "secondly, you should be so lucky Joe Mason!" Will snapped his fingers just to be that little bit extra whilst Tutu lapped up all the revelry his loaded joke had cause whilst others in the smoking area seemed to also be enjoying the exchange. The Southend Scene really did enjoy whatever domestic came their way. Letting himself admit camp defeat this time Joe surrendered with his hands-on full show but still allowing himself to laugh "ok, ok whatever you say Mr. But can we get inside now because I've had my fill of fags for the next hour and I'm sure a certain Queen wants to get her war paint on" Joe indicated a nodding Tutu who seemed to be itching to get in. "Oh yes baby, this one has gotta start applying pronto for the full effect and then some..." Tutu called across his shoulder as he entered the pub in front of the duo, "I see you'll on the stage!" the Drag Queen hollered as the doors closed leaving them both still outside. Letting himself now chuckle quietly Will was glad to see such a person perform; he was in sore need of the distraction from the other stuff he was sure he was bound to witness tonight. Turning to Jo he offered his arm to the door "Ladies first?" Will mocked but Joe took it well "oh don't mind if I do. Those other two will be wondering where we've got too"

Joe lead the way back into the small space and whatever lay ahead for them.

*

10:52 PM...

The Hen Party were fully in to their enjoyment now, the butch lesbians with their so-called cheerleader girlfriends were still commandeering the pool table but no one seemed to care or mind, Tutu still out of full Drag had more or less vaulted through the pub to their backstage area to get ready without anyone taking notice that the entertainment was in the building whilst Johnny and Josh were by the bar with the fourth round in awaiting promptly. After the outside talks Will let himself take a generous gulp of his now third beer which gave him a good buzz when he finally allowed himself a breath "careful Will, you'll be pissed before Tutu even gets up there for her set" Josh chided sarcastically.

"Least I can handle my liquor unlike some"

"Meow, someone's jumpy..."

"Not jumpy just cold"

"And a cold beer is the best way to warm up I'm sure" Josh kept up the sarcasm but Will didn't rise to the silly game his friend was playing since he knew he was just trying to distract himself from having to deal or rock the boat with Joe. Will had seen the looks Josh had been giving Joe since their arrival, of course Johnny didn't pick up on it and he was the one with glasses who was meant to be observing how everyone behaved in this place tonight. Will wasn't so hopeful that Johnny would rise to the task set for him, but they still had time yet. '*Let's hope Johnny will figure out that them two are part of his observations tonight as well*' Will dared to hope some more regardless if it would backfire on him or not. "How's Johnny enjoying the place so far then?" Will directed at his best mate "yeah it's nice" Johnny replied.

"It's just nice?"

"What, I did answer the question?"

"Yeah but what do you like about it though? The people, the atmosphere, dare I say it but are the blokes rocking your boat? I know there isn't much to go crazy over in terms of eye candy, but you never know, slim pickings down here for one thing..."

"I dunno" Johnny mumbled his response with a shrug of his shoulders but Josh then jumped in for the defence "ah come one Will don't be daft there aren't any guys that fit Johnny's criteria for one thing in here tonight unless you count Mike or Carl over there in their little corner" Josh stopped to take a quick drink whilst all three of the boys were now starring in puzzlement at what Josh meant. He finished and looked at the boys like it was the most obvious thing ever.

"Seriously? We all know Johnny's type right..."

Josh let the question hang out there in the open but none of the boys especially Johnny were willing to give any kind of answer, "oh it's so obvious, there aren't even any blokes in this place tonight in the forty-plus age bracket for Jonny to get his hands on!" Josh finished as Will and Jo both doubled over in stitches whilst Josh even let himself enjoy the joke as Johnny stood there bug-eyed thinking it would help him mount a comeback against Josh but nothing of the sort happened. Wiping away tears of laughter Will looked at Johnny who was clearly not impressed still which brought out further laughter which passed on to Joe then Johnny folded his arms in huff choosing to look elsewhere until the boys got over it. Breathing heavily whilst fanning his face Will regained his composure along with Joe, "Johnny you gotta admit it..." Will began speaking as Johnny returned to look this time "but that was a bloody good joke on Josh's part" Will continued to snigger as he clinked glasses with Josh in a very sportsmanship-like behaviour. "Yeah Josh that was a bloody good one" Jo said then planted a light kiss on Josh's cheek before returning to his Rose' waiting on the bar top with his back to him.

Billy Harding © 2020

He didn't notice that Josh lightly touched his cheeky for a very brief but quick second which Will and Johnny saw but as soon as he had done it the next second his hand had snapped away like the act was a figment of imagination on their part. *'Not a good sign at all'* Will made another mental reminder to keep watch on them both even as he polished off his now fourth Corona Extra of the night. "You asked me what I thought of the place" Johnny said which got the boys attention "Well..." Johnny began. "Yes?" the boys said in unison, "well, I like the drink prices" Johnny finished saying as he sipped his Amaretto and Coke whilst it was now the turn of the other three to give him their own version of a bug eye looked. "What? I again answered your question" Johnny stated by returning to his drink once more. Shaking his head in disbelief Will resigned himself to the fact that Johnny most definitely was not following his homework assignment like he should be. "Speaking of drinks I am in need to relieve myself in the little boys room so excuse me lads, back in a mo" Will made his way from the boys to the back of the pub with the task of having to pass by the much more merrier Hen Party that Ryan Tate was a part of. Will noticed that the other guy who was with him was none other than Ryan's boyfriend and of course they happened to be having a kiss much to the delight of the married Bride to be and her group of gal pals. "Wahey that's my mate kissing his fella, get in there Ryan right in with ya tongue babes!" the Bride was clearly however many shots in with no let-up in sight as the ten-strong girl mates all squealed or awed at the kissing lovers. Will would have rather not seen any of it really since Ryan had been somewhat of let down for him. As he apologised when making his way through the Hen crowd, he saw Ryan looking at him as he continued to kiss his boyfriend, rather than stopping Will looked away and carried on to the toilet trying to thinking nothing more of it. '*What on earth was he staring at me for? My receding hair line I bet*' Will thought as he finally got round the bar through the one-person archway to the safety of the toilets where the crowd didn't care if they used the men or women's. It was unisex heaven in this joint whereas other venues would very much enforce the gender rule but not here, here it was a free for all as long you respected one another which was only fair at the end of the day. Gay Bars based out of major city areas or large towns even needed to exist in order to be a real safe haven for anyone coming to terms with their identities so the concept of a unisex policy for toilets was something nobody batted an eyelid too here which was a good thing. Sticking to the norm Will went down a small flight of stairs off to the sanctity of the men's and found it deserted plus a lot quieter despite the ever camp songs being blasted whether they were enjoyed or not. Enjoying the somewhat muted silence for however long it would last he did his business, then as he was finishing the door of the men's opened. Groaning internally at his disturbed peace he turned around zipping his flies up and came face to face with none other than Ryan Tate's smiling boyfriend. *'Holy shit'* Will thought as he placed a charming smile on his face to cover his surprise? "Will, right?" the boyfriend began "I'm Sam, Sam Wight, Ryan's boyfriend. I think we've met a few times here before?" he finished as he went the urinal to sort his own bladder out. Will so far was cautiously relaxing as he went to the sink to slowly wash his hands unsure how to act or if this was some sort of set up, "so are you all enjoying the Hen Party tonight? Seems you're all very much getting on it with the drink I noticed once or twice" Will kept the conversation light as he finished drying his hands whilst Sam had finished at the urinal. Laughing he nodded "oh yeah there isn't gonna be much let up at this rate either" he said as he joined Will by the sink "but it's all good fun in the end before the lucky lady gets married so she has to enjoy her *last night of freedom* as the old saying goes so what better way than to get her plastered in a Gay Pub right" Sam explained as he dried his owns hands, Will chuckled in agreement "it definitely looks like most of us will be waking up and making a beeline for water with good headache tablets no doubt but that's part of the fun isn't it" Will replied. "Absolutely, you haven't been here in a while have you?" Sam asked as he answered a text on his phone, Will was thrown a little by the question yet continued to play along "yeah actually it's been ironically eleven months to the day since I last visited here so it's really good to be back. Staying away I find always makes the heart grow fonder and all that soppy crap you know how it is" Will joked which Sam was once again nodding his head at "I would totally be like that too but the boyfriend always wants to come here so I entertain him every time" Sam replied as he pocketed the mobile, "every time then you say?" Will asked this time genuinely curious "well yeah pretty much, it's fun plus everyone knows each other" Sam answered as he made his way round Will to head back out to the rowdy pub. Will still had his curiosity piqued now however "but just purely wondering of course, doesn't it get boring for you?" Will questioned as Sam gave a puzzled look in return so he pressed on with it "I mean, yeah this place is a laugh when I visit no doubt about that and it's great to visit again for say tonight. I also of course totally understand and respect the need or want to have a regular, but you said it yourself the boyfriend wants to come here *every time*?" Will stopped for a second to see if Sam was catching his drift but he still firmly had a confused look on his face so Will went in with a much simpler line of questioning "don't you want to do anything that you want which might entail not having to come here all the time? Going somewhere else even?" Will asked which seemed to register on Sam's simplicity level. Smiling like butter wouldn't melt the devoted boyfriend with his chocolate brown gelled spiky hair that was easily a good decade out of style by how he had done it now responded in kind "you would think so but that boy of mine..." he stopped for a second looking into a top corner of the toilets with an almost distant dreamy quality on his face whether it was booze related or not "...that boy could do anything he wanted and I would still just be with him for the hell of it. He just sees me you know what I mean. He lets me be noticed from everyone else and it just works for me so I let him do whatever, whenever" Sam paused to Will's fixed face but rather alarmed eyes "He's got me well trained I tell you Will, see ya out there!" Sam finished with another simplistic grin plus a shrug of his shoulders and left Will alone in the toilets. Will stood there in another slight daze looking at the closed men's toilet door for a moment not quite knowing what he had learnt about Ryan Tate's overly devoted beau or if he had learnt far too much of their relationship setup if you could call it that. It was like a plaything that was of interest for a person very much in charge of a one-sided arrangement with no free will ever included for the other. "I don't think you have a single bloody clue what your boyfriend has really done to you Sam Wight..." Will muttered then taking a quick look in the mirror to collect himself "other than obviously neutering you to the point he could literally do anything or anyone and you wouldn't even blink because he is still passing you off as your boyfriend" Will finished his mind-numbing assessment. Taking a long hard look in the mirror Will took notice of his strong jaw line, sky blue eyes, receding hair and five foot, six and a half inches in height. '*Least I am happy with myself but a situation like that? No thanks, I would rather have a good one shag that and be done with it*' he encouraged himself internally. Facing the door to the leave the toilets he went to head back to the boys and whatever else awaited him.

*

11:09 PM...

Tutu still hadn't come on stage and it was now well past show time but the crowd all seemed to be happy to wait it out. In fact, a good majority seemed to be well and truly liquored up so a Drag performance would definitely send most of the audience off the deep end in a rather happy fashion. Having had four Coronas now Will was very much in a happy place himself then Johnny came up to him by the pool table with another beer at the ready, giving him a pointed look which Will didn't skirt around the issue "you're hitting the sauce tonight aren't you bestie?" he asked Johnny who gave his own signature shrug "I did tell you I

like the drinks prices as its cheaper than London"
he replied "yes but any chance you get to be in
central London right now rather than here you
would literally jump at it" Will swigged the drink
then noticed something. "Where are Joe and
Josh?" Will asked as he scanned the pub
meticulously for the other half of the Foursome,
"Joe wanted another cigarette so Josh went with
him outside" Johnny answered but Will's warning
bells were going off in his head already at the
mere thought of them two being alone, especially
with the looks Josh had been giving Jo since they
had arrived. Will then made a point of looking out
the double doors to see if they were in the smoking
area, thankfully he saw that they seemed to be just
talking normally for now. "Phew..." he exhaled in
relief "you ok?" Johnny asked but Will just
nodded his head which was all Johnny needed to
know for now. Placing his amaretto and coke next
to Will's beer on the now vacated pool table, the
butch lesbians had given up their posturing game
at long last Johnny excused himself to the toilet
leaving Will alone. As his best mate left Will

busied himself on his phone little realising, he had been joined by another individual until he noticed a figure just standing near him out of the corner of his eye. Looking up Will once again maintained a cool exterior but was flipping out inside at the person in front of him. It was none other Ryan Tate with his Hen Party sash hanging exactly right off his left shoulder and a full-on smirk in place as he looked Will up and down with only the movement his eyes studding him. He hadn't made any sort of greeting so Will feeling out of sorts began for them both, "Ryan, hey good to see you" Will smiled nervously unsure of what else to say or do whilst Ryan with his pointed nose, dark brown almost black hair along with a set of some dark piercing eyes still probed Will non-verbally for another moment. He finally responded with what could only be classed as a naughty smirk "yeah it is good to see me isn't it Mr, you look good I must say. How's life?" Ryan looked around the Gay Bar absentmindedly treating Will very much like he was part of the furniture. Still no clue as to why he had come over all of a sudden Will played along for the moment "yeah life is ok I guess, not been here in while and I saw Tutu would be performing tonight so I thought a special trip was in order. See you're having a good night with your Hen Party?" Will indicated the sash which got short laugh "yeah it's not so bad these kind of parties, gotta all let our hair down. You don't ever come down here often do you...that's a shame" Ryan waved at his boyfriend Sam who was laughing and joking with the Hen Party at the bar, he was also indicating another shot in his hand that was obviously for Ryan which he acknowledged with a one minute gesture. Will was still staring at Ryan in complete confusion at where this unexpected conversation was even going '*what are you even doing talking to me right now Ryan Tate? We flirted, you sent me a picture of your pert naked ass over WhatsApp when you were very much single and fancy free then you expected me to make all the effort even though we could have met up in the city since you work there*' Will thought as he sneaked a cheeky glance at his still impressive behind which Ryan saw him do but didn't say anything about it, he seemed to enjoy the attention really. "It is a shame really" Will began which seemed to finally grab Ryan's attention "that we never got to meet up for...well *you know*" Will tilted his head to one side but didn't go as far as insinuating or saying something that would cross a line but Ryan was completely with him now.

"Yeah it is a real shame"

"Agreed"

Ryan then made the conscious effort to look Will directly in the eyes and took one exceedingly small step closer to him with an almost seductive velvet tone to his voice "but we still could?"

"What..."

Four

The Pool Table.

11:25 PM...

Will blinked.

Then he blinked some more.

Ryan simply continued to stare at him directly in the eyes like they were connected and was breathing heavily for just a moment, then without uttering another word walked back across the other side of the pub from Will to his boyfriend who was still waiting with the shot, downed it in one then planted another generous kiss on his unsuspecting lover. Will just stood there shaking his head numbly. Ryan stopped kissing his cleverly deluded and oblivious boyfriend flashed one more look at Will with that same stare full of insinuations then returned his full attention to the Hen Party. Allowing himself to finally breathe at last, Will let it out like he had been holding his breath underwater for that little bit too long *'what the actual fuck just happened?'* Will looked at his Corona numbly like it would talk back to him with a valid solution. Whilst everyone went about their business in the pub no one paid him much attention, Will then marched over to the bar far away from Ryan Tate and his provocative intentions, he got Sophie's attention and ordered not one but two shots of Sambuca downing them in quick succession. The well-known vicious substance was sickly strong and felt like a very potent liquorice was making its way down his throat and helped to numb Will even more from what had just transpired with Ryan a few short moments ago. Returning back to the still vacant pool table with a fresh Amaretto and Coke for Johnny as well, Will carried on with his vacant look into space as his best mate returned. "What's the matter?" Johnny asked placing a hand on his shoulder as Will handed him the drink without responding at first, shaking his head and then returning back from his confused thoughts Will drank his beer before finally speaking "let's just Johnny that this night is opening my eyes to *a lot* of different behaviours I had forgotten about" Will didn't elaborate any further, not yet anyway. "Well as long as you're going to be alright?" Johnny rubbed his back reassuringly which Will nodded vigorously to "yeah, yeah I'll be ok. Cheers" Will raising his beer to clink with Johnny's mixer who returned the gesture in kind. Relieved that his best mate was with him Will enjoyed himself as he felt the alcohol finally starting to hit him, especially the two shots he had downed to help the process along. All he needed was a Drag Queen to complete the night. Then Sophie got the microphone out again *"lads and lasses get those drinks in because Son of a Tutu will be on stage in just ten minutes, yes this time she will be gracing us all with her presence finally after the small delay you don't wanna miss it!"* Sophie signed off to a few woops and cheers and like loyal punters some of the crowd with the Hen Party cleverly front and centre made a thirsty beeline to the bar with the butch lesbians not far behind either. Joe and Josh had come back from Joe's cigarette break; both seemed fine but Will even in his much more alcohol-infused state of mind could tell Josh was a bit on edge than usual, *'oh great what happened there then'* Will kept note of Josh as he got the round in. "You alright Sullivan?" Will asked as he nudged his friend while they waited to be served, "yeah I guess" Josh said quietly without glancing at Will *'ok this is gonna either stay the same or turn worse very quickly'* Will looked at Josh's face and found nothing to help him there. He had a fixed neutral look which gave literally nothing away making Will's job working out what had happened with Joe all the more difficult, "you wanna talk about it Joshy?" Will kept his tone playfully light nudging his friend again but he got a single shake of his head in response '*shit*'. Knowing it was better to leave well enough alone Will didn't try to pry out anything more from Josh about what may have happened between him and Joe outside in the smoking area. Joe however wasn't with Will, Johnny, or Josh; he was talking to Mike Harkness and Carl Simpson near the DJ booth at the back of the bar. '*Double- shit!*' Will thought as he clutched his sixth or seventh Corona which he now intended to make last for a while, taking a quick breath he made his way over to Joe and the two self-entitled deities. Of course, they were holding court at their table; this was their turf after all and Will didn't understand why people would let themselves become like this in such a small scene down in this backwater town. He understood the nature of supporting one another which he did admire that about the pub that it stood for that reason but the status that Mike and Carl had carved out for themselves over the years they had frequented this place was somewhat of a mystery to him. Truth be told Will really didn't want to ever find out why they held on to this so-called status, *'leave well enough alone I say'* Will surmised as he finished the small journey over to their table by the DJ set up. Mike and Carl were in their element chatting away with Joe but having that slight distance between him and them, highlighting an obvious divide if anyone who was still sober enough to take notice of it. Funnily enough Joe was right in with the duo as they sat atop on their thrones or glorified bar stools bizarrely to Wills observation as they took notice of him. "Will!" Mike flung open his arms to give Will a hug "so good to see you. Sorry I didn't say hello earlier, but we had to do the rounds you see with some of the regulars, you know how it is" Mike released him. Mike was tall blonde portly fellow close to his forties but not in them yet with a charming smile in place but a set of deep piercing eyes that didn't miss a beat, he may be paying to you attention but he was fully clued up in everything else going on around him as well. "Ah I know your popularity here in this place Mike, no need to apologise for it you sly dog"

Will countered the charm Mike was exuberating with the same amount back at him so he would be appeased plus he added in a wink which got a relaxed chuckle *'first one down. Now onto oh great...Carl'* Will prepared himself for take two. Carl Simpson was another one who had very much solidified his base at the pub over the years by forging a friendship with Mike early on; this easily dated back a good decade and a half of dedication to one another. Of course, they always made the masses that had come and gone from the pub feel more than welcome but they had properly woven themselves into the very fabric if not DNA of the Gay Bar with every management or owner it had changed hands with. Surprisingly to Will he was still short of amazed why the two friends hadn't taken up to running the Pub themselves if they cared so deeply about it or they were just truly content after all these years to so subtly continue their manipulations to get their way. Get their acts booked, get their celebrations organised before others, get their friends or shags priority at the bar, get any of their discounts ahead well before anyone else had the better idea to try and beat them to it. The longer you showed up to a certain venue or made it look like you *actually* cared that was small enough and amenable to your ways of thinking the more easier it was for them and this duo, well they were in there with a vice grip and not letting go easily. No wonder Will played nice rather than pushing against them, the pavement outside would be a welcoming spot to deposit him if he crossed these two. "Well hello there Carl" Will began as Carl turned his head in the direction of Will like he had now become of interest to him at his own leisurely pace, Carl Simpson was an entirely different story when it came to Will yet also quite similar to how he conducted himself in the pub. *'Despite how you treat me Carl, you're still bloody good looking'* Will begrudgingly admitted it to himself. Carl and Will had, had an on-off attraction over the times they had seen one another in the pub or when holidaying in Gran Canaria when it hosted its own Pride event in May time but it was always typically when it suited Carl yet Will had allowed himself to be treated that way. *'I'd rather you than Ryan at least'* Will checked out Carl up and down making the guy fully aware he was doing it, Mike his loyal wingman as always watched with one eye whilst continuing his chat with Joe never missing a beat. Enjoying the attention on him Carl allowed himself to respond "well, well Mr Will. Finally decided to come pay us a visit or were just hoping I might be here?" Carl then gave Will his own casual once over assessment. Carl was in his mid-thirties but looked younger than that easily thanks to a very useful injection of a certain substance in the face once or twice in his lifetime that he talked about openly, he was decked out in what could only be described as smart-casual which he fully knew just how well he pulled it off; he wore some tartan trousers that clung to his legs just the right way to make them look like they were toned underneath with a simple black button up shirt that made his shoulders look nice and broad with a matching velvet waistcoat to boot, plus his brown hair may have been gelled and spiked typically like the turn of the century styles but he pulled it off far better than Ryan Tate or his boyfriend Sam possibly dreamed they ever could, the hierarchal pecking order had to be maintained after all. Carl was aware he had dressed to impress and Will would've let him do whatever he wanted to him then and there if previous behaviour wasn't stopping him in his tracks, he knew better than to give in so easily to baseline instincts in a place where people would almost jump on a scandalous moment whilst also tearing large chunks out of fresh gossip like that. Oh yes Mike and Carl may have differing styles or looks, Mike keeping the outfit choices to simple blue colours and plain jeans along with comfortable trainers while Carl kept it unique with splashes of colour plus proper loafer shoes but you knew exactly who they were, not to be messed with. Will decided to play along "you think I came all the way down here *out of my way* just to see little old you Carl Simpson?" Will countered.

"Well did you Will? I am one of a kind after all"

"What do you think?"

"That's for me to know and you too..."

"*Not* find out. Bitch?"

"Come on now my boys!" Mike tore himself quickly and almost too easily away from Joe whom he left hanging in mid-conversation like it was a magic trick to intervene by putting a hand on each of their shoulders "we're all friends here after all. Let's play a bit nicer, shall we?" Mike squeezed each of their shoulders steering the conversation into calmer territory but kept the control in his court. Carl shrugged his shoulders uncaringly and returned to his drink whilst scanning the pub for anything that would take his interest other than Will. Shaking his head in surrender Will gave up too "it's good to see you again regardless of any *past tension* Carl, you look good by the way also..." Will let the peace offering hang there but all he got was a side eye glance as he took another sip of his alcoholic beverage. Will turned away without any further conversation happening between him and Carl *'and that's one of the reasons why I don't come here often even if*

Carl is easy on the eyes, now what were the others?' Will asked himself in his alcoholic infused state as he went over to re-join Johnny and Josh back at the pool table while Joe continued his clearly one-sided chat with Mike who seemed to get more out of letting him speak for his own personal amusement. "What's Joe talking to Mike about?" Josh asked without looking at Will "I dunno, beats me" Will shrugged in response looking at the last vestiges of his beer left in the lukewarm bottle which hadn't lasted for as long as Will hoped but Josh was adamant now by getting Wills attention, "you mean you didn't even listen in to their conversation while you were over there?" Josh was asking rather quickly now with widened eyes which he found alarmingly odd of his friend.

"Why would I intentionally listen in to a conversation I'm not a part of Josh?"

"Well you normally do most other chats"

"Maybe yes but there's a time and a place for that surely?"

"You just don't know thought Will. Look at how he's speaking to Mike like that..."

Will turned around to appease Josh even if he himself saw or felt nothing out of the ordinary with Joe and Mike simple talking however one-sided it was from Will's own observations only a moment ago. Turning back to face his old friend he placed a sympathetically calming hand on his arm to stroke it whilst looking at him in the eyes, Johnny knew better for once than to keep quiet for something like this. Will decided not to hold back "Josh what's going on with you two? Clearly you're both in different places mate" Will kept stroking his arm to be soothing but Josh was just shaking his head profusely, "nothing alright it's just I want Joe around us tonight and not anywhere else" Josh decided to look into his Coke a Cola like it was a bottomless ocean but even Johnny wasn't convinced now. "You do seem like you want to keep Joe closer to all us though Josh. Like you don't want us to lose track of him" Johnny said but Josh wasn't even letting him off the hook "oh don't tell me the quiet one is now taking a side!" Josh deflected which made Johnny's signature bug eyed look spring forth once more "*what?* I'm just saying that's all".

"Funny how you strangely found your voice all of a sudden Johnny"

"Well I was only pointing it out"

"Yeah well keep it to yourself since you're really good at that..."

"Oi, come on now Josh. Your mates are worried about why you're obsessing over this, what do you even call Joe these days anymore?" Will leapt into Johnny's defence but Josh was now in full shutdown mode. "Don't worry ok. I'm going to the bog" Josh finished by stalking off to the relief of the toilets away from the two very confused members of the Foursome. Looking at each other Will and Johnny were only further confused by their friends alarmist mood swing. Looking once again as he finished of the dregs of his beer and noisily put it the bottle on the still empty pool table, everyone else in the pub was wrapped in their own business having not even taken an interest in the lad's turn of events. Johnny looked at the empty bottle Will had deposited "another?" he asked his best friend, having lost count now but all of a sudden having been sobered up by the last few moments Will was ready to return to that special numb place alcohol permitted you to go. Nodding his response for another Joe then decided to return to from his chat with Mike "how are my queens? Where's Josh?" Joe looked around for his on-off beau if that were a fitting description to sum them up, "bog" Will, and Johnny said in unison as Johnny headed off to the bar. "Ah ok, I am so ready for a spot of Drag now" Joe was fidgeting about like he had itchy feet "how did it go with Mike then?" Will enquired. "Oh, Mike's lovely, always gotten along with him. You know he's not bad looking even if a bit older than Josh but there's nothing wrong with an experienced mature man now..." Joe then went off in his own tangent discussing the pros and cons of Mike as Will stood there nodding his head slowly when the realisation was starting to sink in. Joe was exploring his options tonight at the pub all in front of Josh to see. His very friend he had shared a bed with however many times *'he's probably even got Grindr at the ready'* Will just realised then as if it were now his own individual magical moment right there out popped Joe's phone from his pocket with a very blatant Grindr message having come through on his notifications. *'Fuck me sideways'* Will was now internally in the same state of alarm just like Josh had been a few minutes ago, then low and behold Josh decided then to return from the toilets. Joe quickly stowed his phone away acting like nothing had happened and Josh hadn't seen or if he had he didn't let on to the fact. "What are you all up too?" Josh began "just waiting for you Mr" Joe answered like butter wouldn't melt "ready for a show? I know I am" Joe continued his fidgety routine which puzzled Josh to no end, Will for once kept his mouth firmly shut but his mind

was very much in overdrive *'this night literally
just keeps getting better and better doesn't it? One
of my close friends is still pining for his former
flame whilst the guy in question is clearly looking
for some fresh meat to sit on and my mate is still
under the impression there could be something
between them yet little does he know...'* Wills
thoughts were interrupted as Johnny held another
new beer close to his face, he also placed a pint of
water with some ice down on the pool table too.
"You know what I'm gonna say don't you?"
Johnny let the rhetorical question hang there, Will
put the beer down picked up the pint of water
without saying a word whilst never letting his gaze
leave Johnny's probing face. He took a generous
swig of the ice-cold water which felt good to drink
other than gassy beer. "Thank you" was all Johnny
said in return whilst Will just harrumphed. Then
the speaker system stopped playing for a moment,
the crowd started cheering and wolf whistling in
the silence, then the new music began to play
replacing the tired camp tracks as reliable as they
were. The lights dimmed and the double doors of

the pub entrance swung open again letting a small gust of chilly wind in. Son of Tutu then re-entered the Gay Bar dolled to the nines with a fabulous headdress in place and her show finally started. Only just about one hour and twenty odd minutes later than it was meant too.

Such was showbiz life for a Drag Queen with a popular fan base.

*

11:54 PM...

It was the timeless Alannah Myles classic *Black Velvet* as Tutu's opening number, the Drag Queen made her way through the awaiting audience who cheered, whooped, and clapped her on to the stage that was now hers. She took it like it was only hers as well. Will and Johnny had their phones out at the ready recording the moment.

"Mississippi in the middle of a dry spell

Jimmy Rogers on the Victrola up high..."

The crowd swayed and cooed along with singing, the butch lesbians were feeling it immensely with their girlfriends and some inappropriately placed hands.

"Mama's dancing with baby on her shoulder

The sun is settin' like molasses in the sky..."

Sophie and the bar staff even got in on the action and started to enjoy the music Tutu was singing which had the crowd enthralled. Playing to her strengths to a well alcohol fuelled audience in a Gay Pub would get anyone in there ready to dance to a self-confessed power ballad. Some members of the Hen Party were loitering around at the front of the stage very much enjoying the show more than any normal person would, but Tutu didn't let that faze her, she was a professional through and through.

"Oh, I love this Drag Queen so much don't you...?" Will turned to look over his shoulder as he recorded Tutu perform on his phone to Joe and

Josh to find they weren't there; in fact, it was just an empty space where they had been standing.

"Where'd those two go?"

"Where did who go?" Johnny responded turning as well to find his own question answered immediately for him.

"Oh..." was all he said.

The two guys looked at each other for a quick moment and simply shrugged their shoulders returning their full attentions as to why they had come to this pub in backwater Southend tonight and leaving whatever was going on with Joe and Josh to fates own hands. For now, that's all that mattered to them. Tutu was now approaching the chorus to the crowds continued delight as they also continued to dance or sing along with her, well and truly under her musical spell.

"Always wanting more, he'd leave you longing for

Black velvet and that little boy smile

Billy Harding © 2020

Black velvet and that..."

Then all of a sudden, everything changed in a heartbeat.

"Off my stage you SKANK!" Tutu bellowed into her microphone.

Five

Down the road.

12:02 AM...

Josh was walking.

No, he wasn't, he was frogmarching for all his worth.

Joe was following him uneasily somewhat behind him. Josh didn't even know why he was walking so fast away from the pub or why but he needed to do something with Joe out of reach from the

'Southend Lot' who would in a heartbeat ingratiate themselves in their business if him and Joe began an argument right there and then on the pub floor. He knew better from that crowd than to involve anyone else except just the two of them right now. Even the mere thought of any gay guy, lesbian or whatever the hell they identified as these days giving their unwanted opinion turned Josh's stomach in knots. No this was for him and Joe only, the others including Will and Johnny could be damned if they thought their comments could help right now. *'How the fuck am I gonna say this the right way?'* Josh thought with no actual viable option springing forth to help him, *'fuck it'* he decided as he turned to face Joe who was still keeping a fair bit of breathing distance between. All Joe knew was Josh had asked him or more specifically told him that they needed to talk right now, and he had near enough pulled him outside the pub without anyone surprisingly even noticing as Tutu's set had begun. Now here the two men were on a deserted street up from a gay bar in a backwater town of the county of Essex with nothing but atmosphere and silence physically separating them for the moment which as about to change for better or worse. Taking a slow breathe Josh went for it.

"What are we doing?" He asked Joe who simply stood there quietly.

Joe blinked and made a pointed look at Josh as if he had actually lost the plot, "Seriously?" He responded looking around them as if the answers would fall out of the night sky itself. "Well currently me and you are stood here in Southend slowly but surely getting colder by the minute" Joe gave an answer but intentionally avoided Josh's face who at that moment had raised his eyebrows clearly more than dissatisfied by what he had heard. Letting out an even more obvious frustrated sigh Josh became more emboldened whilst Joe just stood there meekly, "Look, I like you Joe ok. We've sort of been working our way through this as we go and yeah we've have a good few laughs along the way as well as a few good shags I'd say so..." Josh paused for a moment but Joe still just stood there as if eternally waiting for the penny to never drop, Josh pressed on "...but what we've been doing these last couple of months I've really enjoyed but we've never actually spoken about or even broached the subject of *what we actually are*" Josh stopped as Joe's facial features started to change. It was the realisation of it all. What Josh really wanted to speak about and Joe only seemed to coming round to the idea now after all this sequence of playing the innocent act, *'you really haven't been paying as much attention to what we have been doing with one another this whole time whilst I have been playing it over and over in my head'* the sickening thought flashed in Josh's mind clear as day but as soon as he had thought it into existence he squashed it like the annoying bug it was, no weakness on display here, only purposeful intent.

"What do you expect from me Josh? I agree on the fact we've been having a good time lately" Joe shrugged his shoulders not giving anything away which only stoked the fire already burning hot in

Josh's heart even more. "Come on Joe, I have been on this merry go round well before you came along into my life. Even when I use to try and tell myself I was *straight* for all those years, then I started living my truth" Josh was almost pleading with Joe to open his mind up to how he was feeling. It wasn't just this small moment for Josh however, when a younger guy finds someone like him attractive just the way he is it changes you, it makes you feel something you thought you weren't anymore. Desired. For Josh this was something he needed to get off his chest with Joe before it ate him from the inside out.

"So, your saying that what we've been doing is something, what *more*?"

"You tell me Joe, please enlighten me..."

"I still don't know what you want me to say?"

"Ok. Start with how you were talking to Mike just now in there" Josh indicated back down the road to the pub where Tutu's set could be faintly heard in the distance. Both were secure in the fact that no local gays would be loitering about to eavesdrop or unless they had found a good-looking male victim ensnared to take down an alleyway for some adventurous fun before rushing back for last orders in at the bar. Being such a small scene down here the gays took their thrills when and where they could not take into account any decorum, no time for that when horniness beckons. Joe was still at a loss but was also alarmed *'oh crap he saw how I was interested in Mike. Ok relax, I'll play the dumb act for as long as I can'* Joe prepped himself mentally, but he also didn't want to string Josh along since he thought of him as a nice guy anyway, "look Josh..." Joe began as well as taking one step closer to Josh "that was nothing with me and Mike. We just get on, you know what it's like with someone of his status in these parts" Joe even gave a small flourish with his hand back to indicate the pub even though in his thoughts he spoke a different story *'yeah ok I would have it off with Mike a few times if I'm that lucky for sure, if it gets me some collateral in that place I wouldn't say no. Besides whom hasn't used sex for power once in their lifetime. Plus I'm cute as hell'* Joe kept up his pretence by stepping a little closer to Josh but he was on guard still "Joe you are younger than me I admit that and I know others in life wouldn't agree on an arrangement like what we have had", Josh still kept trying to get through to Joe as he came closer to him now resting both his hands on Josh's shoulders in an understanding almost sensual way nodding as if he really understood what Josh was saying. "But can we not try? Just try to maybe be something a little bit more than two friends who have had a good few fucks? Try to spend time making each other..." Josh was stopped as Joe then kissed him without warning. It wasn't a shocking kiss, but it was tender yet considerate. Josh then put his arms around Joe's waist reciprocating the kiss, intensifying it which Joe enjoyed even more in the moment. *'Now this is what I like about him'* Joe hungrily thought as the passionate subterfuge went on *'yeah ok there is some truth to what he is saying, I have enjoyed him that was never a something I doubted really. But I am young and I want more than just this, I need more than just this really, I need more Daddies other than him'* Joe stopped the kiss and the two guys just stood there in the embrace for a pregnant pause breathing deeply having both enjoyed it in equal measure yet for differing reasons. The subterfuge seemed to have won over Josh at least for the moment who still quivered a little as Joe tussled his hair with one hand while stroking the back of his neck with the other very slowly. *'Damn, I think I'm better at this than I first thought, I bet Carl and Mike would be proud of how I can manipulate something to get what I want'* Joe guessed as he finally let go returning each of the men to a less heated state than before. Josh then leaned against a nearby car for support staring at Joe some more, *'crikey he does tick my boxes but even I know he has done that just to get me turned on and less focused about what I want for us both. I'm wasting my time and Will would even tell me so'* Josh let that miserably honest fact hang there in his mind to focus him once more as Joe flashed another

cheeky grin like he had still won then we was
distracted by his phone which he pulled out of his
pocket. "Who loves you on your there then?" Josh
asked as he stopped leaning, "oh my girl mate just
text me that's all. She's asked me to crash round
hers after I'm done at the pub with you guys..."
Joe said without looking up from his phone as he
typed in his response. Josh kept his face in neutral
which he could do well on any given moment even
if he still wasn't letting Joe know right away that
all was said and done with the both of them, in fact
Josh had a pretty good idea about who had really
text Joe. "So which guy has shown you some
interest on Grindr then? Josh went in without
warning as Joes head snapped up from his phone
eyes wide in shock.

"You think I am actually on Grindr right now after
what just occurred with us?"

"Well, are you?"

"Josh, I think I have made it clear to you already
about us..."

"Without going into *any* specific detail about what you really want of us in the same instance"

Now it was Joe's turn to let out a frustrated sigh. *'God I give him the attention he asks of me then he wants that little bit more still'* Joe kept looking at his phone then he gave up and passed it with a roll of his eyes to Josh who took it from him gingerly to inspect the contents, Josh then let his shoulders relax fully. There clear as day on the screen was a message from Joe's girl mate with the promise of a meet up after his night had concluded with the Foursome at the pub, Josh felt instantly like he was back in school having been pulled up for being an immature misbehaving student. Locking the phone and handing it back to Joe who deposited it away he crossed his arms with a piecing look at Josh. "Sorry. I just wanted you to really understand how I feel about us" Josh muttered as he looked at the pavement in defeat whilst Joe kept his arms folded "and so you instantly think I am searching for that next shag like I get bored that easily do you?" Joe kept up the pressure on him, "well clearly I made a mistake when I assumed you were on Grindr just now" Josh glanced a look at Joe who seemed to accept this as the apology he wanted to hear. "Yes well, making assumptions about even talking to anyone other than you or the boys tonight is all I'm allowed to do these days Mr. Didn't realise I was your property?" Josh unfolded his arms but kept the tone pointed.

"You're definitely *not* my property"

"Could have fooled me after that little stunt you just pulled"

"I have just stood out here in the cold trying to convince you what I really think about us haven't I?"

Joe then decided to soften his features just a touch as truthfully, he was moved a little by Josh's overture as both guys missed out on Tutu's ongoing performance in the pub whilst they debated back and forth in the chilly night air their difference of opinions. *'Despite what I really think he does have the best of intentions. It's also annoying too when I know what I want and I want to simply have it all on my terms while I can, just gotta say or do the right thing when it comes to him'* Joe gave Josh an up and down appraisal with that raised eyebrow look he knew he did so well then once more closed the distance between them again planting a light kiss on his awaiting lips. "I guess I'm gonna have to put up with you a bit more aren't I then, *Daddy*" Joe teased Josh who then raised his own eyebrows in surprise.

"Honestly, Joe? You mean that?"

"Well, I did just say that didn't I? As long as you let me crash at my girl mates down the road after we're done with the lads tonight?"

Josh nodded his approval and gave Joe another kiss which he allowed. Satisfied Joe then started walking back down towards the pub with Josh following, his phone then vibrated again in his pocket. He slowed his pace as Josh overtook him turning back once again to face him, "your girl mate making sure about later? She is up late as well I've just realised..." Josh said as he looked at his own phone "...since its already 12:40! Damn no wonder we aren't colder, the boys will be freaking out about getting a lift back from me if we don't get back in there to join them soon" Josh pocketed the phone then rubbed his shoulders quickly for a bit more warmth. Joe was nodding as he looked back up from his phone "oh bloody hell yes your right, tell you what I'm gonna give her a quick call and I'll meet you in there?" Joe offered as he put his phone to his ear. Josh now fully at ease even if they hadn't delved as far as he would have like into where they both truly stood with one another was nodding too "yeah, yeah I'll see you in there in a couple of minutes" Josh turned around to keep walking then stopped, he turned back to Joe again one final time who was still waiting for his girl mate to answer the call.

"Hey, are we gonna be ok after this Joe?"

Joe took the phone away from his ear slightly; smiling innocently as he simply nodded then flashed his cheeky grin again. "Yeah, yeah forget about it see you in a few" he responded then walked away a little with his phone back in place. The boys parted opposite ways then as Josh reached the pub again Joe snuck a look back over his shoulder happy that he was alone if he was now well and truly cold from the weather. He brought the phone away from his ear and returned to his message from his girl mate he typed another text back to her:

Hey queen! Listen I'm gonna stay at Josh's tonight but we'll just rain check for another time, peace out xoxo 00:42

He sent the text off.

Then Joe went and opened the Grindr App. There waiting when he opened it was an unread message from a rather attractive forty-something man without a name on his profile other than his nickname he had given himself on the hook-up app, his profile information was straight to the point as well:

Silver Daddy. 43.

'Looking for that younger man to help his Daddy out tonight, any takers...'

Ethnicity – White

Body Type – Muscular

Position – Vers Top

Tribes – Twink

Relationship Status - Single

Joe had seen the notification come up when Josh had correctly guessed that he had, had someone message him off the app. Luckily before he handed over the phone, he had closed it and got rid of the notification. "What's a guy to do when he has a list to pick from right at his fingertips?" Joe asked himself aloud as he opened the unread message, the guy on Grindr had been conversing with Joe sine he had got to the pub and now it was getting to the juicy stuff much to Joe's horny delight. He'd even sent a few snaps over to whet his appetite even more and Joe decided to relent and returned the favour with a few suggestive pictures of his own, even the particular favourite jockstrap he was wearing underneath his clothes tonight:

"Damn boy, you ready to take all this?" 00:45

Grindr - *Picture Received* **00:45**

"Mm, you might be surprised *what* **I can handle..." 00:45**

"Oh yeah? Wait till you see what I can do!" 00:46

Grindr - *Location Received* **00:46**

"See you later then! Probably looking at a 2 arrival though..." 00:47

Grindr – *Picture Sent* **00:47**

**"Worth that wait if you ask me boy, this *Daddy*
is in need of servicing!" 00:47**

"See you then. *Daddy*. ;)" 00:48

Joe closed Grindr more than satisfied with how the
events had turned in his favour now.

Not bad for forty-five minutes worth of innocence
and placating to add to his list of improvisation
skills. *'Just get this done then it will be time for
some well-deserved new Daddy action, I can't
wait!'* Joe thought gleefully. Yeah, he did like Josh
that was never out of the question, but Joe wanted
more and tonight he was getting just that. The
thing he loved about the app was the experiences it
offered to you once you have gotten chatting to
that new guy, the app had changed the very
dynamics of how the Gay Community viewed and
conducted itself to this day. Sure it brought
everyone closer to talking or hooking up if you
fancied it but it had replaced the very much tried
and true method of needing to physically go out
and hope on that one particular night out that was

when you would meet the one. The one guy who would make your night all the more memorable for the both of them. Yes technology had changed the very nature of the game of chase and elevated it to a new digital era at the turn of the millennium and people like Joe fully benefitted from its continued existence, whether it was good thing or not is all down to any guy's taste level. For now, though Joe was playing his own naughty game whilst having his cake and hoping to eat it too. Placing his phone back in his pocket he smoothed down any creases in his shirt, took a deep breath in, rubbed his hands together and exhaled then made his way back to the pub to whatever else was going on. Tonight, he was making his own rules, and no one would tell him otherwise.

'I really hope my hip action is still good when it comes to riding fresh meat...'

Six

Back Inside.

40 - 45 minutes earlier...

12:04 AM.

"Get your FAT ASS off my stage!"

Some of the crowd laughed in hysterics whilst some had to scrape their jaws off the floor. The bar staff including Sophie were looking from one another like a rapid-fire game of tennis with no discernible outcome. Tutu however was not impressed by the turn of events. One of the Hen's from the Hen Party had decided to just sit on the edge of the stage to look up at the Drag Queen as she started her opening number; evidently Tutu was not impressed one iota.

"Get your fat ass OFF!"

The audience along with Will and Johnny were beside themselves at the audacity of the drunken Hen overstepping her mark. The *Black Velvet* soundtrack kept on playing but Tutu had very much lost her place on the track having to still deal with her unwanted guest in her personal space who she now finally had standing again after muscling them off the stage.

"Stop the music!" Tutu commanded from the stage, signalling the DJ Booth operator who was scrambling now over the controls.

"Stop the music!" She gave another blistering command and the music ceased while most of the audience were in stitches, the butch lesbians were

rolling over each other having to be propped up by their girlfriends. The bar staff were still frozen in their places unsure whether to intervene or not. The audience started to calm themselves but were still sniggering as Tutu dramatically placed one hand on her waist and looked at the clearly swaying Hen Party member directly in the eyes, Ryan Tate along with his boyfriend Sam were beside her now looking nervously from the Hen to the Drag Queen none the wiser as to what was about to happen.

"What the *fuck* was that?" Tutu deadpanned into her microphone without looking away from the drunken Hen as the audience once again swelled up in heaps of laughter, this Queen was definitely not to be messed with. Will was wiping away his own tears of laughter at the turn of events whilst Johnny was transfixed to the spot his phone not having missed any of the last few moments as he recorded it all. Tutu however was not letting her victim off the hook just yet.

"Do you think it's a *homeless shelter* or something?" She gave the still swaying Hen an up and down judgemental look, the audience were still covering the mouths in hilarity or shocked amusement for equal measure. The Hen then started to respond with her hands as Tutu allowed her to speak into the microphone for the first time.

"I'll just...get you a suitcase or somethin'..." the Hen incoherently answered as Tutu raised her eyebrows, taking the microphone back to her mouth, she paused for a bit more of dramatic effect then gave the awaiting audience what they wanted.

"You see..." she looked at the audience in the small space "...I don't talk *idiot!*"

She proclaimed with her free hand fully raised letting the Hen know she was being shut down very effectively, the Hen placed her hands on her own hips still clearly intoxicated as the audience were still enraptured by the highly unscripted moment. Tutu now had the crowd well within her element pressed on "when you go to the O2 Arena to see someone like *Rihanna* or *Adele* do you think they let you sit on their fucking stage..." the audience let out a big ooh at this but Tutu went with them, "I know I'm no *Adele* or *Rihanna* but this stage deserves the same respect *right*!?" She was now looking into the crowd who were all cheering their agreements with her. Turning her attention once more back to the Hen who was now being covered more flanked by Ryan and his boyfriend Tutu then reassuringly softened her stance, "you just stand there and..."

"No respect for you!"

 The DJ had hollered from the booth at the back trying to catch Tutu off guard midsentence, but she was ready as ever "no respect either for you *bitch*! Ha-ha-ha..." Tutu became more relaxed along with the engaged audience as Ryan tried to persuade the Hen to come back to the bar, but Tutu had one last piece of advice to give. With another reassuring free hand and the microphone still at the ready like a weapon, the Drag Queen made full use of her moment, "you just stand there my dear and respect that this is my stage or *there's the fucking door*!" Tutu flourished to the ever-waiting double doors and the crowd backed her up with more cheers, clapping and wolf whistles as Ryan successfully pried the Hen Party member away from the stage and Tutu's commanding presence. Satisfied with herself that she had rectified the situation with some well-deserved ritual humiliation she indicated to the waiting DJ and *Black Velvet* began playing from the start. The crowd now eating out of Tutu's palm began their enjoyment of the music also, the butch lesbians took their girlfriends in overly loving embraces, the Hen Party steered well clear of the imposing Drag Queen which was the best decision they had made that night, Carl with Mike had not missed a beat of the drama sitting ramrod straight from their thrones at the back with mildly amused expressions and Sophie with her bar staff knuckled down double time to taking drinks orders once more. The pub along with its current residences settled back into its designated loops or narratives just like it was almost a programmed status quo was expected of everyone whilst Will and Johnny kept to themselves like strangers as they recorded Tutu on their phones. '*One quick moment to disrupt the normal behavioural pattern then it's back to what they all know*' Will was observing the crowd '*how repetitive they all are. Do they all just come out to live for small moments like this? Lap up the drama then revel in it for all its worth?*' Will found the questions he was asking himself sat uneasily in his mind, he didn't care for it at all. In fact, he damn well didn't like this pattern of behaviour all on show before him one bit, to him life wasn't meant just for this kind of stuff, there was far more to enjoy than that. "No wonder I..." Will stopped muttering to himself as he was saying it louder for Johnny to take notice who also looked at him in confusion, "you ok?" his best friend asked.

"Yeah, yeah bestie sorry. Just tired tis all"

"Ok, long as you're sure?"

"Yeah sure am! Fancy a Coke, I'm laying off the alcohol for a little bit..."

Will moved off to the bar without Johnny openly responding to take a breather as Tutu was hitting the chorus of her opening number:

"Black velvet and that little boy smile

Black velvet and that slow southern style

A new religion that'll bring you to your knees

Black velvet if you please"

Most of the crowd were singing along, all save the Hen Party that seemed to be in the midst of damage control as the Hen who had made the grave mistake of sitting on Tutu's stage was being reprimanded by none than the Bride to be with lots of finger pointing and hand gestures for added measure, all very much being refereed by Ryan's overly dutiful lapdog boyfriend Sam while Ryan had removed himself from the situation to sip a drink at the bar as he scanned the pub seemingly disinterested in the mediocrity encompassing the Hen Party for the time being, like he was above it all. Ryan's eyes then laid upon Will at the far end of the bar who had been staring a bit longer than normal himself as he waited for his Coke's and he was once more giving Will that same piercing look from earlier that made Will feel very much like a fine cut piece of meat on display, ready to be eaten. Ryan and Will continued their eye contest until it was broken by Sophie noisily placing two pints of ice-cold Coke on the bar top, gratefully drawing Will's attention away from those eyes.

"Ah cheers Sophie, how's the night going for you all?" Will enquired to the blonde bar manager who still seemed to have the energy of a lot of the twenty-something years old in the pub and her staff included even though she was well past forty, a good looking one, nevertheless. Shrugging herself she came across unbothered.

"You know how it goes Willy boy; this is a typical night for us down here"

"Even with moments that happened with Tutu and the Hen?"

"Oh yeah. This is a Gay Bar; you know how it is? There will always be someone trying to upstage the other..."

"Of course, I get that, but a patron disrupting the performance of your hired act for the night?"

Will took a generous swig of the Coke which felt good down his throat after all the beer, granted Coke is also gassy but the sugar fix kept him more alert than bubbles. Sophie wasn't one to give much away about earlier but she entertained Will some more, "between you and me Willy if that Hen had stepped out of line even a toe more she and her *entire* party would have been gone out those double doors quicker than you can say thank you for the music, god love ABBA and all" Sophie stated matter of factly.

"Including Ryan and his fella?"

Sophie paused for a moment; the question seemingly throwing her off guard which Will knew wasn't an easy feat. *'Got you there didn't I Soph'* Will surprised himself as Sophie glanced down at the still bickering Hen Party. Reverting her eyes back to Will she took a quick breathe "Well, I will say this. Ryan is obviously a regular in this place and yeah he is part of that party just for tonight but..." she paused again trying to find the adequate words; Will waited patiently not wanting to press any further than he already had, eventually she responded. "I suppose when it comes down to it I can make exceptions, Ryan has brought money into the bar for us which is a good thing no doubt so I wouldn't throw him out but them lot..." Sophie used only her eyes to indicate the party "out on the street, bye, good riddance" she finished with another simplistic shrug.

"What if I was part of that party tonight Sophie?"

Will waited for the response knowing it was an unknown gamble, but he wanted to know the hard truth of where he stood in this place, Sophie stared right back at him not missing a beat. "Oh, Willy boy, you would have to go with em babes, just *business* you see at the end of the day..." Sophie called out as she made her way to next waiting patron taking the cash out of Will's hand as she went. Will stared after her not sure what to think or feel from the loaded response Sophie had just given him so calmly. It had so many meanings to it even if the way she delivered it as innocently as possible *'guess I really am the outsider when it comes to this joint after all. Of course, she would back up that slag over there though, that attractive slag...'* Will let the thought trail off to himself as he re-joined Johnny who was still recording Tutu who was now well into her second song with a jubilant crowd enthralled, *'she would actually kick a kind-hearted person like me just for being part of a party with one disruptive person out the door but let one of her mates stay? Guess it really is all about who know in this joint with conceited friendships taking a precedent'* Will took his chance to actually look at the pub now as he handed Johnny his Coke who thanked him in kind.

The pub itself was for a better word in need of a lick of paint or two for that matter. Its walls were a simple boring cream colour to make the space seem bigger than it was but the carpet was in dire need of being pulled up and replaced all together, Will could see it coming away from the walls if you concentrated on the corners. *'No wonder the drink prices are cheaper the further out from the City you are. Guess freshening the place up isn't the top priority since it was exactly the same when I was here eleven months ago'* he noted to himself as he returned his attention to more of Tutu's set, she was now onto her own rendition of the *Body Rockers* hit song I Like The Way You Move but the lyrics the Drag Queen were using were hers and she had some of the local lads up front but specifically not on her stage keeping the control well within her grasp. Johnny was sniggering along to Tutu's clever use of suggestive lyrics:

"And I love to go down and LICK their big hairy balls

And I love the way they love to touch

And I love the way they SMELL so much!"

Tutu was touching the biceps and shoulders of all
the boys she had at the foot of the stage who were
trying to keep themselves from creasing up once
again, they were however failing rather epically to
keep their cool which only made the Drag Queen
enjoy the attention more. Will forgot about
everything for a moment to take it all in, the
music, the atmosphere and trying to not keeping
lingering to the thoughts in the back of his mind he
still had that he didn't feel like he was entirely
welcome here in this place. Like he was that shiny
new plaything for one night only until none of
these people all barring his friends, he was with
would make an effort with him once he walked out
those doubles doors again.

"I LIKE THE WAY YOU MMMOOOVVVEEE!"

Tutu's vocals brought him back into the here and
now as the crowd went wild for the chorus of the
song dancing wherever they pleased; even Carl
and Mike were bopping along despite not having

moved from their thrones. One of the butch lesbians had then decided to just all of a sudden mount the pool table to make a statement of how much she was really enjoying herself as Will and Johnny stood there with gaping mouths at the sight developing in front of them. The butch lesbian in question had whipped off her chequered shirt to wave it around her as white vest clearly showed off for all to now see she didn't favour wearing a bra underneath as her girlfriend and mates egged her on. However, someone was ready to handle this, Sophie came frogmarching out from behind the bar with a face of thunder in place. "Right you, off the pool table, *now!*" the bar manager had her most severe voice on, but the lesbians girlfriend was trying to cover for rebellious lover, "aw please she's only having a laugh! She'll be down in a minute" the girlfriend made the pitiful defence for her woman blocking the way and Sophie didn't budge an inch on the matter by squaring her shoulders more.

"Fine, if she's not gonna move then we can certainly do something else can't we!"

Sophie then took the girlfriends elbow firmly in her hand and through sheer will power had the girl out of the double doors of the pub before anyone else could even react. As if on cue the butch lesbian still mounted atop the pool table froze while looking at the doubles doors Sophie had exited with her woman in tow, leaped down and flung her chequered shirt back on legging it after her girlfriend with her mates in hot pursuit. Tutu, the audience, the bar staff, the boys, the Hen Party, Carl, and Mike, all were frozen to their respective spots as well. Tutu's track had finished. Everyone stared at the double doors which then opened suddenly, and everyone collectively gasped then let out a disappointed groan in the same instant. It was just Josh having returned from outside. He looked round at everyone in the pub as they stared back at him, dubious as to what he had done Josh only did what he thought was appropriate, "what did I do now?" he asked everyone looking at himself as if he had something on him that was unpleasantly fascinating. "Nothing Josh, get over here" Will beckoned his friend over who happily obliged not questioning any further as most of the crowd still stared at the double doors. "Care to feel me in Will...?" Josh asked confused as everyone gasped again as the doors flung open this time it was Sophie having returned, seeing the attention on her she raised both her hands in mock surrender. "Don't worry all! I sorted it look at me, not a scratch in sight, them lot out there wouldn't dare touching a hair on this head if they ever wanna get back in here..." Sophie twirled patiently so everyone had a good look at her; Tutu still on the stage finally moved her microphone her mouth. "Well everyone, now we know who to call to sort out any unruly *muff munchers*! Let's hear it for Sophie!" Tutu flourished her free hand to the bar manager who made a quick bee line to get back behind the bar as the audience gave Sophie a rowdy round of applause from Tutu's well-timed cue. Laughing it off in style Sophie made a motion to the DJ who got some music going promptly on the sound system while the Drag Queen kept the audience's attention for a moment longer, "well ladies and gents that was the first part of my set. That was a turn of events ah? But now this queen right here needs a good stiff JD and Coke if anyone wants to buy me one and a ciggie, I'll be back in twenty or so minutes for part two, be ready my dears for some more camp antics!" Tutu signed off to whoops and cheers as the double doors of the pub opened again with Joe walking in to re-join the Foursome. Looking somewhat crestfallen as he came up to the guys, he watched Tutu leave the stage to go talk to Sophie behind the bar. "Don't tell me I missed Tutu; I was really looking forward to her!" Joe folded his arms sulkily as Josh put a reassuring arm around him but introverted Johnny was jumping in at the ready "oh no don't worry we have another set from her coming up soon" Johnny stood beside Joe patting his arm which he brightened up too that he hadn't missed out entirely. "Oh, thank god, I was getting worried then" Joe put a hand on his chest in a mock campy fashion which Josh chuckled at whilst Will didn't miss the reaction from his friend. '*Those two patched things a bit up I see, rather quickly too*' Will made a mental note, "so what did we miss then?" Joe asked as he flagged down one of the bar staff for another round of drinks "well the better question is what *didn't* you miss" Johnny chimed in as he took his new Amaretto and Coke off Joe which got him looking even more inquisitive. Will chuckled at Johnny's sly dryness then came in to back his best friend up.

"*Basically*, you missed out on not only Tutu giving a crowd-pleasing first set but some unplanned drama as well"

"What drama was that then, nothing bad with Tutu I hope!"

"Yeah, even I noticed the mood when I came in as everyone eyeballed me" Josh said.

Will and Johnny laughed collectively amongst themselves for a moment at what their friends hand missed. It was always fun filling in the blank spaces your friends didn't know. "Well..." Johnny continued "some lesbians decided to take things into their own hands" Johnny took a swig of his beverage as Josh was waiting with baited breathe but Joe seemed to know where they were heading.

"Oh, that explains so much from outside then..."

Will, Johnny and Josh all looked at Joe confused who was staring into the distance vacantly. "Explains what?" Will asked now that he was in the dark about something Joe knew then turned his attention fully on to him.

"Well the lesbians, the butch ones with the lady friends, right?"

"Yes?"

"Well..."

"Well what?" the boys said in perfect unison all wanting to know the gossip Joe was now privy too. Some apples don't fall far from the forbidden tree when you're Gay after all. Joe waited for a moment to find the right words, and then he had them. "Well, they were all literally shouting over one another in the street like they were about to tear chunks out of each other, no one was taking responsibility for whatever the other had done" Joe answered with a shrug the waiting boys without looking at them. The lads all looked at each other then at the double doors, low and behold the butch lesbian and her girlfriend were out in the road shouting and gesturing for the whole world to see. The rest of their group had dispersed, off to their homes more than likely or to try it with another bar or club if they would admit them at this late hour of the night. Shaking his head Will looked to the bar at Sophie who he managed to catch her eye briefly then used his thumb to indicate the two left outside, all she did in return was make a quick cutting motion across her neck shook her head and got back to serving the thirsty patrons pumping money into her till. Sniggering quickly at the response despite her earlier treatment towards him Will polished off the reminder of his pint of Coke only to see Joe had gotten him another Corona

Extra. Just looking at the cold beer made him need the toilet, so he excused himself for another round trip to relieve his bladder. Entering the toilets he was glad to see it was still empty for now so he enjoyed the muted noise of the pub in the background and did his business at the long continuous urinal, he even closed his eyes for a moment taking a deep breath willing himself to relax. *'Fuck I am tired and it's just gone...'* his fished his phone out of his pocket to check the time *'bloody hell, it's gone 1:15!'* he was surprised where the time had gone, had him and the boys really been in the pub for over four clear hours. Work had drained him enough with all that was going on there then he had decided to come for a night out with his lads and now Will was really starting to feel it, he hoped they wouldn't be out for much longer now in all honesty. Thankfully, he knew he could crash at Josh's back in Basildon then head home in the morning, since Josh wouldn't need much persuading anyway. Will had closed his eyes again after looking at his phone which he deposited back in his pocket; he zipped his flies up when all of a sudden, the toilet door had opened once more, his short peace disturbed. His eyes snapping open at the sound he made sure his modesty was all secure by looking down quickly. Turning one hundred eighty degrees around he readied himself to go wash his hands with a semi-smile plastered in place to acknowledge whoever had entered the toilet as well. Good manners cost nothing in this day and age after all. Then Will's semi-smile was wiped off his face in an instant to be replaced by a more shocked jaw hitting the floor as he still had one of his hands firmly placed on his crotch area frozen in place. Standing in front of him was none other than Ryan Tate who had a rather ravenous look on his face, especially in his eyes which he didn't hide or even attempt to mask. Ryan's eyes slid down to Will's hand on his crotch then back to his still jaw dropped face. Will finally came to his senses shutting his mouth as his bodily functions returned to him, Ryan then took a step closer narrowing the gap between them like he had done briefly earlier. He was breathing heavily, even more intentionally now.

"Please..." Ryan began "...don't be shy around me; I've seen it all before on WhatsApp, haven't I?"

Ryan took Will's hand which was limp for some reason away from his crotch area, only to replace it with his own hand in kind. He then began rubbing the area in a very meticulously slow fashion, the heavy breathing continued, and he got himself even closer into Will's personal space. Will was somehow still frozen but was now all of a sudden breathing heavily himself from out nowhere. *'Why the hell am I breathing heavily along with him? Fuck, this shouldn't be happening...'* Wills alarm bells were going off in his head but no one at this present moment was coming into the toilets to rescue him. Ryan had increased the speed of his hand rubbing and down there in Will's crotch he was now becoming excited from the attention, he was damn well near enough fully hard which Ryan enjoyed more so as his heavy breathing quickened whilst rubbing even harder.

"Ah, I didn't know you cared *that much* Will"

"Err; this really shouldn't be happening..."

"Shouldn't it? Your referring to my boyfriend out there in the pub, aren't you?"

"Well who else would I be referring too...bloody hell I am now literally *throbbing* down there!"

"Mhmm yes you are, excellent!"

"No, no not excellent. Bad! Very, very bad!"

Will was still frozen in place not touching Ryan but simply not moving. Ryan had now placed his free hand gripping tightly onto Will's left shoulder which kept him in place with surprising strength considering Ryan had quite a stick figure about him. Will resorted to closing his eyes tightly to try and block it all out then Ryan removed his hand from Will's still incredibly excited crotch along with the other one too. Exhaling loudly Will kept his eyes shut for a moment longer. Opening his eyes slowly Ryan was still there right in his personal space, but his heavy breathing routine had stopped, all that was left was his eyes, those deep piercing set of still attractive eyes bore into Will for all they were worth. All Will felt was alarm with a tinge of embarrassed excitement which he knew he shouldn't be feeling right now. *'Please, please just stop being hard. I'm still throbbing and he's not even touching me now!'* he was desperately trying to command his crotch into submission, even looked down at it with wide eyed shock to see the bulge there on full display for the world and its mother to see. Will could practically hear the judgments raining down upon him. Ryan looked at the bulge too. "You know what I think Will?" Ryan now closed the gap leaving no space between them.

"Wh... what?"

"I have a name you know"

"What *Ryan*?"

"I think *Will*...you need to just shut the fuck up!"

Ryan then grabbed Will's crotch once again like a vice which throbbed even harder at the renewed attention whilst simultaneously grabbing the back of Will's neck with his other hand, then Ryan Tate and Will Hardley were kissing all their worth, inhibitions could go to hell for them.

Talk about a turn of events.

Judgement was raining down on both of them.

The crowd out in the pub were none the wiser either.

Seven

The Self-Entitled Throne Area.

25 Minutes Earlier...

12:50 AM.

Carl Simpson observed the underlings as they all mulled about.

Yes, he looked at them liked that because they were just that too him. Royal subjects and he was the Queen who ruled over them, at least for tonight anyway. Sure, he was friends or acquaintances with some of them, but he knew his place here and he could do whatever he wanted, when he wanted. All it had taken was one simple thing which was time. Time had in turn rewarded him in kind, status in a place that he could do what he liked. Not that he took advantage of that earned status. Of course, there were people in this place who he didn't associate himself with on a regular basis; they needed to know sharing time with him was a very precious commodity; it was a real experience and privilege after all. Hence why he knew he looked good tonight in his tartan trousers that he had a real affinity for, particularly as his rear end stood out well in them. He hadn't moved from his regular spot after he and Mike had entered the pub but the looks some of the other guys visiting tonight had been all the validation he needed and knew he could get. It made him feel sexy even if he was fast approaching his mid-thirties, an age in the Gay Community that was viewed as highly undesirable or as some others would put more bluntly, dead. Oh, Carl knew here in Southend that he could do things down here that he necessarily couldn't do in the city, if he ever went there often he would just be another one in the millions of people going about their business all in a rush. No down here he was a Queen to be reckoned with and he used it well just like his best friend Mike Harkness did too albeit in his own way. They just had different approaches to how they utilized that status and tonight Carl was very much looking for a good hard screw, not that he gave any of that sexual intention away. No, he was a classy bitch after all. *'Whose cock will I be sucking and bouncing off tonight if I can be bothered then?'* Carl mused to himself scanning the room for any viable candidate that ticked his boxes. He stopped at one grouping as one individual had, had the nerve to come over to him and Mike earlier which he sort of admired as convoluted as it was, but he found that same nerve they had shown to be also distasteful too. *'You come over to mine and Mike's personal space then you won't be staying for long, not unless you really piss me off'* Carl looked at the group which was Will, Joe, Johnny and Josh. Carl inspected them all with a very well used neutral face that gave nothing away even to any other guy who may have been checking him out at the same time. Carl appraised each of the boys who were chatting amongst themselves. He judged Joe and was immediately putting him in the *never-to-shag list* he had stored in his mind. Carl was just shy of six foot tall which was a good height to be but Joe he noticed was taller than him, thinner than him, lankier too, curly mousy brown hair, dressed head to toe in black clothes and literally might as well have screamed at the top of his lungs from the rooftop of the pub that he was more than likely a screamer bottom when he took it the right way. *'Nope, never, next'* Carl moved on to Johnny *'hmm not bad, he definitely hides behind those glasses of his though, he should be much more confident because of his height however'* Carl looked up and down at the shy boy taking his time. Johnny he noticed was near enough the same height as Joe but he held himself completely differently, less folded arms and much better posture with differing shades of blue along with converses that actually suited him plus some well styled hair that didn't move because he had obviously used a shit tonne of hair spray on it but Carl appreciated it more because he used probably same amount on his hair with gel to boot. *'Not a bad bubble butt either in those tight jeans'* Carl noted as he stole a glance then stared a bit more just knowing where was situated on his table was the right vantage point. Glasses or no glasses Carl gave Johnny a mental tick of approval and moved him in to his list of guys he *would or might shag*, keeping his options open on the metaphorical table in his mind. Next up was Josh who spoke for himself with plain non-designer branded clothes and trainers whilst being second shortest in height at probably a good five foot ten or eleven, *'nice chest, good to get a hold of if you're on top of him, thick arms, be good to lick those biceps if you fancy it or if your into that sort of thing'* Carl kept his mental assessment going as he was handed another beverage from one of the bar staff who personally delivered it to his and Mike's table whom he did not need to thank. The staff member wordlessly walked away, sipping his chilled double vodka, lime and lemonade Carl enjoyed the taste and how no one disturbed him. Mike his wandering best friend was once more chatting to people in the pub, one of the Hens from the Hen Party. Carl couldn't help but give a little smile for his friend, he genuinely enjoyed chatting to people even if it was to mine whatever fresh gossip they had going on or anything he needed to be made aware of so him and Carl could stay well above the curve of any unexpected or upcoming changes. *'Forever protecting us aren't you my dearest Mike'* Carl approved affectionately of his friends intentions even if he didn't show it, he represented the half that had basically kept them safe and secure in the pub after all these years, Carl was the face and body of the duo while Mike was unseen hand working tirelessly behind the scenes. It was a greatly beneficial and cooperative friendship that had stood the test of time so far. He was definitely not giving it up any time soon that's for sure. Carl finally then turned his observational eye onto the last member, Will Hardley himself. Shortest out of all the boys at a petite or average stature depending how you looked at it five foot six or seven Will had gone for a grey long sleeve t-shirt and black jeans combination look plus he was the only one who was wearing boots out of his group, suede grey ones as well to match the grey shirt. *'Good styling'* Carl began then he stopped for a moment on his once over of Will, Carl found himself admiring this guy somewhat more than Johnny or Josh. In fact, Carl would probably even say what a cutie he was. Carl intentionally took a long sip of his drink whilst staring fully at Will's pert behind in his black jeans, sure the black hid it well but Carl had skills of his own for seeing the outline of it, it excited him a little as he indulged his wandering eyes. Carl snapped himself out of his naughty ways and then began to reassess Will in his usual clinical way *'nice legs in those jeans but next to nothing on mine, good set of blue eyes, broad shoulders, receded hair but it suits him I guess, wander how much he is packing down there?'* Carl without moving was able to get a side eye crotch view of Will and he didn't find anything too damagingly big, *'it's never about the actual size but how you use it, I should know for one thing'* Carl sniggered at his own internal joke as he polished off the beverage then simply raising his glass to the bar staff who was more or less his designated waiter clinked the remaining ice in the glass like a bell. The member of staff raised a hand in acknowledgement then began preparing a fresh one for Carl to consume. Carl was satisfied with Will or Johnny if he would even choose either of them as he knew Josh and Joe was definitely a thing by their general close proximity to one another, *'I'll let the Daddy one have his way with that thing or whatever he is'* Carl mentally placed Josh in his *never-to-shag list*. "You win some you lose some..." Carl muttered aloud as Mike finally returned to their designated table having successfully wormed his way from the Hen Party member who clearly liked to chat a tad too much as she was looking at Mike's back like she was a pining dog awaiting for her master to return. "Took your time I see?" Carl noted with a singular raised eyebrow of the Hen who was still waiting, Mike just chuckled "put your claws away Simpson she's a nice girl who...", "you're getting the latest news out of. Yes, I know you, remember?" Carl finished the sentence as he took his latest drink from the male bar staff, but Carl then grabbed his wrist all of a sudden who looked at Carls hand then to his face. Mike watched the unexpected exchange occur between Carl and the member of staff. Carl looked at the staff member in the eyes, he rubbed the guy's wrist lightly but almost sensually then he gave him a noticeable wink whilst releasing his wrist back to him. The staff member was blushing a little then smiled whilst looking Carl up and down, then without a word went back to work as Sophie hollered for him from behind the bar. He rushed off whilst Mike gave a low whistle of approval.

"Another notch on the bedpost tonight Carl?"

"Just keeping all of my options fully open Mike..."

"Yes, I see that. Does that explain why you were staring at Will for tad longer than was actually required a moment ago?"

Mike grinned with his overly white teeth cheekily while his friend gave him a side-eye look refusing to cave into the joke he had thrown. "Like I said. Options." Carl responded dryly then took a nice gulp of the alcohol which felt good down his throat, Mike was ready to tease and probe his friend further however "so that longer than usual stare at Will was nothing to do with say...reminiscing about Gran Canaria back in May this year?" Mike asked. Carl still kept his cool exterior attitude fully alert.

"I honestly don't know what you mean by that?"

"Well, you have to admit by the pool there were some staring back then as there are tonight, granted it's rather one-sided because that lot over there have no idea that we're talking about them right now..."

"Again, I'm missing your point to a holiday that happened almost over five months ago now" Carl answered as if butter wouldn't melt when truth be told he had, had a little flashback moment when staring at Will a moment ago. Mike Harkness was not only a constant presence here at the pub but he also organised holidays away for a big crowd of the regulars he was well ingratiated with, granted of course they all paid for themselves plus bring their own spending money on top, but Mike had chosen to invite Johnny and Will to Gran Canaria and they had gratefully accepted. Will had attended with Josh in the previous year as well, again at the courtesy of Mike except of course this year when Johnny came along. In May, each year the island hosted a nine-day Pride event and Mike had been attending ever since its inception when it started out as just an evening event with a singular large tent. Skip forward a few years and it was now a fully established Pride which brought in thousands of people from all over the UK and other European countries, so over the times in the past Will had visited with Josh to the pub Mike had of course gotten in friendly with them both plus vice versa so being invited on a holiday by Mike was inevitable eventually hence how they had ended up discovering the wonders of Pride abroad. Last May had come and gone yet Mike was still very much in the dark about Will and Carl or if anything had occurred between them, he didn't even know any detail which was strange for his friend not to divulge the juicy facts.

Carl's little flashback moment purely consisting of Will in a particular way continued. "So Mr..." Mike carried on with his tongue in cheek playfulness distracting his friend again "...what really happened between you two? He did make an effort to come earlier to say Hi bear in mind" Mike tried the guilt tactic but if Carl felt anything below the surface, he certainly wasn't showing it in his face. His forehead hardly quivered in fact. "Let's just say my lovely Mike; I am just remembering how much of a *pervert* I am when relaxing by a pool" Carl finished answering resorting to a staring contest with his friend whilst finishing off his vodka, lime, and lemonade. Mike who couldn't do staring contests for love nor money just laughed admitting mock defeat, raised hands and everything. Out of nowhere came a little noise of attention and Mike turned his head to see one of the Hens had now resorted to tempting him back over with the promise of a shot waiting in her eager hands as she jumped up and down like a lost little puppy, Mike sighing but also keeping the smiley pretence up gave his friend his own brand of a side eye glance signalling he needed help of getting out of this but Carl ever the dry one simply gestured for him to head back over to his fan girl, shaking his head while laughing Mike departed to accept the shot and whatever conversation he was about to be subjected to whether he liked it or not, Carl smirked at his departing back as he went. Ritual humiliation wasn't just for the Drag Queen who happened to be booked for tonight. Carl returned his gaze and attention to his previous activity of analysing the Foursome without physically moving his head which was an art form in itself. They all chatted amongst themselves like a motley crew with Will very much steering the ship, Carl did find Will rather intriguing. He found his confidence to be his most alluring feature, sure he was not what you would call one of the best-looking guys around, but he made up for it in other ways, his personality. Carl rather enjoyed how he treated Will aloofly *'doesn't mean I wouldn't say no to a couple of rounds in the sack, however. Bet he is one little pocket rocket when he gets going'* Carl continued studying Will's attributes' as another vodka, lime and lemonade was deposited like clockwork on the table by the unspoken barman who was now just standing there with his hand still around Carl's awaiting drink. Carl decided to touch the barman's wrist again the same way he last had, then he found himself entwining his fingers slowly with Carl who decided to give this audacious guy his attention since he was very much risking the wrath of Sophie the bar manager who could really crack the whip when she wanted too by trying to just get Carl to notice him. Looking at the barman he found a very specific smile, slightly taller than Will but not by much, some nice dirty blonde hair spiked with wax, a set of probing green eyes along with an up and down appraisal look which then lingered on Carl's signature tartan trousers that he had thankfully kept cross-legged. The barman was a confident one no doubt as he placed his other hand very lightly on Carl's knee as he was testing the waters. *'Damn your trying you luck, aren't you?'* Carl was genuinely impressed, but he still refused to show it, he never showed any form of weakness or chink in his armour in the pub, ever. Carl then decided to reward the still unnamed barman whom he hadn't bothered to learn his name despite being in the full knowledge the barman knew who he was through Sophie being his boss. Carl's reward was a simple gesture with so many levels of meaning to it. Using his crossed legs in his gorgeous trousers he used his leg foot and began stroking the inside of the barman's right leg, at first the barman just glanced down with his eyes not to make it obvious to anyone else at what he was doing then he opened his legs just a touch wider to give Carl more freedom to utilize which he did. Carl indulged him by stroking his right leg in a much more obvious fashion which drew a very small but controlled laugh from the barman. Taking one last look over the barman's shoulder as he was positioned perfectly between the Foursome, so he had his back to them whilst fully facing him, Carl let his thoughts linger just for one quick moment more on Will one last time this evening. *'Oh Mr Hardley, that time in Gran Canaria was fun when you and I found ourselves in mine and Mike's apartment just the two of us but like all good things, it's always at my beck and call. It'll never be you in control when I deem you worthy to take me to a bed for a good seeing too. That day will come but you're definitely gonna have to work hard for it and I'm still happy to wait...'* Carls thought was interrupted as the barman gave his knee a gentle squeeze bringing him back into focus, Will was resigned to the past for now as Carl's latest notch for his bedpost made his mark on him. *'Let's see what skills you have to satisfy me tonight if you can Mr Barman'* Carl noted as he continued his naughty but excitable inner leg work.

Carl Simpson maintained his status in the pub that night, no one would question it.

For now, they never did.

*

1:05 AM...

Mike Harkness admired his best friend from afar as he worked his sexual magic on the barman.

'Go got get him Carl' Mike thought approvingly. Any of the people he knew of who could nab a good-looking guy like Carl had Mike cheering them on from the side at any given moment. Mike liked Carl's removed attitude to it all, he could even see how Carl would probably be performing later with the conquest, on top and very much letting the barman be ridden for all his worth. *'I don't think that guy has any idea the type of night he is in for with my best mate'* Mike's wicked thought flashed through his mind with a visual image of a very surprised barman flat on his back with shocked ecstasy plastered in his face as Carl took him to new levels of pleasure. Mike was equal parts proud whilst equally perverted and he

was not ashamed of it either, nothing wrong with a little bit of imagination at the end of the day. Besides, Mike knew he could do what he liked here in the pub hence why he had suggested to the owners to book Tutu down from London for a one-off gig to get the punters in, plus throw in a room for the Drag Queen to spend the night in upstairs after she was done with her set and despite the late hour when the pub at this time would be a bit more quieter than usual the crowd had stuck around for the Drag Queen even if Sophie had thrown out the lesbian contingent for the foreseeable future. Mike was kind of glad to be rid of the Hen as well who had been chewing his ear off about which of the other members of the party she was with had been trying cop off with anyone who would show them attention, truthfully Mike was too polite to just shut down a conversation like that, not when he could use information like that to his advantage if any of the Hens chose to step out of line once more in the future if they graced the pub with presence. All Mike would need to do is get Sophie to one side or out back of the bar area and their fates would be sealed if they ever wanted entry into the venue again. Mike would have a polite smile along with a glass of wine at the ready whenever or if ever that situation would arise, this was in theory his place despite the unspoken set up and that's how he always liked it. *'Just call me Cersei Lannister'* he mused as he continued his observations around the pub. The Crowd were liquored up despite it had gone past one in the morning, the pub would probably have everyone carted out of here no later than two thirty even if they had a late license in place that said they could stay trading till three max. Sophie however had probably got the takings to a good level to justify the slightly earlier finishing time plus Mike wanted his bed, Carl would have crashed at his but he was still having an intense eye contest with the barman so that was one less thing to be concerned about as he would find himself in a different bed tonight now. The Hen Party were probably not far off the next lot to be thrown if they weren't careful, the lone Hen who had sat on Tutu's stage was now only being served water by the staff after

the Bride to be gave her a dressing down followed
by a profuse apology to Sophie who had deemed
they could stay with a simple nod of her head,
Mike however had got the bar manager's attention
with a simple look which was him shaking his
head very slowly but Sophie had this time let them
continue as they offered pay for another bottle of
Grey Goose Vodka and promised to let the bar
staff keep an eye on it so Sophie relented, another
fifty quid in her till and sales was nothing to ever
complain about. Lord knows this place needed the
money to stay operating being one of the few Gay
Bars in this part of Essex, if they didn't have this
place who would any of them be without it, Mike
knew the answer to that and it secretly filled him
with dread. He needed this place as much as it
needed him so he did everything he could to keep
the pub alive and trading. He would continue to do
it with every fibre of his being if he had too.

Mike saw Ryan Tate holding court well without
having to do much at all, Ryan just kept close to
the Bride to be who evidently loved having a Gay

friend as arm candy to show off plus to have his boyfriend or slave Mike dutifully noted as an additional was a bonus to any girl group, they lapped up their Gay mates. Mike however had noticed Ryan's wandering eye over to none other than Will Hardley and his group this evening. Specifically Ryan had acted like he wasn't obvious but when you had been around the block more than once in Mike's life you developed keen senses or just noticed as you got older than being part of the Gay Community there was certain behaviours that never went out of style no matter what ever decade you grew up in. Ryan was practically screaming cheater vibes off of his person and Mike found the glaringly obvious gossip just exactly what he needed if Ryan ever punched above his station as he had tried to do in the past several times. Mike however found the power grabs more amusing than anything; it showed him that Ryan really needed to hone his skills a lot more. Mike was the scalpel; Ryan was a hammer with zero articulation.

It was the way Ryan tried to start the odd rumour around the pub. There was no deft or sleight of hand to it just blatant name dropping. One time about over a year ago Ryan had tried to adjust the boundaries of the status quo in his favour and Mike had counter moved on the same night which in turn got Ryan barred from the pub for an easy six-week period. His sources had informed him that Mr Tate was going stir crazy not being allowed admittance into a place he had been attending for years but Mike had told Sophie to keep the order in place until it had expired fully so she had of course obliged Mike first. Once he had come back after his penance Ryan had fallen back into his rightful place which was beneath him and Carl, *'and the status quo was maintained'* Mike let the pleasing thought soothe him as the Hen Party continued in earnest.

Ryan kept his eyes firmly on Will who was deep into his chat with the other lads so was none the wiser of the increased attention on him. *'I wonder if Mr Hardley is fully aware of how desirable he actually is when he chooses to grace us with his presence'* Mike wondered as he followed suit with what Ryan was doing and had a good observation of Will. Mike couldn't deny the attraction of him, shorter but full of confidence, he was by no means a stunner, but he was definitely well placed in the high-end cute bracket which did wonders for him. Sure, his hair was receded, but it gave him his own distinctive look that was all his, nice posture, a good set of shoulders on him, an ass that looked rather tasty for a tongue to explore not just easy on the eyes. Oh yes Will Hardley was a unique individual who could pull all sorts of guys without even knowing it, Mike Harkness included. The once over ended as Will excused himself from the floor to head off in the direction of the toilets, Ryan was watching him as he went all under the watchful observing eyes of Mike who was practically giddy with excitement at what he knew was coming.

Mike kept his posture casual as he leaned on the bar with a drink well placed in his hand then he saw it, Ryan left his Hen Party group and made an all too obvious beeline in the direction of the toilets. The group of Hens and Ryan's boyfriend Sam were all in different states of alcohol-infused fun to even notice his departure from them. Sam was practically starting to sway from one side to the other Mike glanced over which fuelled an idea. *'I couldn't do that, could I?'* Mike asked himself then he shrugged his shoulders then dived headfirst into his idea.

Signalling Sophie, she came over promptly.

"Yes, Mike babes, what do you need?"

"Ah Sophie, you know I love you dearly..."

"Spit it out Mike I ain't got time for arm-twisting. I can practically hear your brain cogs whirring from across this bar top" Sophie deadpanned Mike with that classic dead in the eyes face off which made Mike laugh nervously. "Ok you got me, I need a round of Sambuca shots for the Hen Party, wanna congratulate the Bride myself you see..."

Mike upped the innocence factor by clear ten, but Sophie was shaking her head at this point.

"You know I am *this close* to asking them lot to clear outta here like I did with those lezza's earlier Mike..."

"Ah come on Soph, so one of them stepped out of line. Tutu more than handled the situation with em and everyone else thought it was riot..."

"Still though Mike..."

"You've got what, an hours' worth of trade left at best? Your turning down a good fifteen to twenty quid's worth of shot sales I'm about to sink into your till?" Mike even batted his eyelids as he flashed a wallet full of cash with fresh notes sitting there waiting to be dropped into a waiting till, Sophie rolled hers in response, a sale was a sale after all. "Fine" she relented and went to set the shots of the vicious substance on a small serving tray "but this their last round of shots then they can stick to normal drinks only, I am not having a

single member of my staff cleaning up any
unwanted sick tonight if I can help it, I want them
to their homes for at least a bit of shut eye before
we open up on Sunday. In fact, it is already
Sunday the 16th *officially*!" Sophie hollered with
her back to Mike over the music. She didn't need
to turn around to know Mike had his hands held up
in a satisfying surrender of acceptance. *'Nothing
like a compromise'* Mike paid with his cash as
Sophie handed the tray of shots over, she glanced
over at Carl and Mike's designated table and then
raised her eyebrows as her member of staff was
still rather engaged in a sexual eye contest with
Carl who was still working his magic with the
barman's legs, this time alternating between the
two and the guy was literally quivering with
excitement. Still holding on to the tray with one
hand while Mike had hold with his own, she
looked at him probing his eyes but Mike again
raised his free hand in surrender again at the
unspoken command from the fierce bar manager.

"I'll pry your guy back from Carl's grip, sorry."

"Thank you, Mike," Sophie released the tray and then went over to other waiting patrons. Mike intentionally passed his and Carl' table and made a noticeable noise of disturbance at the two flirty men. Carl's concentration of getting his shag tonight was broken by Mike's interruption.

"What is it?"

"Sophie needs her man back..."

"We're a bit busy at the moment"

"Carl. It's a not a request Mr..."

"Hmm, fine then" Carl stopped his leg work as the barman gave a disappointed look as his now obvious bulge started to go limp which only amused Carl more who decided to something he didn't normally do, he kissed the barman very lightly on the lips then more or less pushed him away with a hand letting him know he was done for now.

Billy Harding © 2020

"Don't go far you; I need to get my mouth around whatever's in those jeans later tonight..."

Carl then went back to his drink not looking at his newest notch who gave him a hungry look of appreciation then scampered off to do some more work. Mike laughed at Carl's who looked at his best friend inquisitively.

"What?"

Nothing, just you, ya little slutbag!"

"I'll take that as compliment, then shall I?" Carl called after Mike who carried on walking over to the intoxicated Hen Party. "Ladies and *gentleman*?" Mike made his presence known as most of the group turned to him. "Where's the Bride to be...ah there you are!" he found the Bride who had only just noticed Mike with his offering of more alcohol "I thought I would bring you a little treat my dears to say good luck in the upcoming nuptials" Mike offered the tray of shots to the group who all took one each excitedly, Sam included. Mike raised his shot to the Bride.

"TO THE BRIDE TO BE!"

Mike and the group all downed their shots, and it had the desired effect he wanted on Sam who began to sway from side to side even more obviously, Mike got an arm round him to steady him. "Little Sam! How you feeling, where's that boyfriend of yours got too?" Mike squeezed Sam's shoulder who looked up at Mike clearly drunker now because of the higher alcohol content in Sambuca. Mike had rather conveniently not touched his own Sambuca shot which he held out to the still swaying Sam who took it greedily and downed the second shot which had the desired effect Mike was hoping for as the boyfriend began swaying even more.

"So where has RYAN got too Sam?"

"I...err...hick...dunno...hick!"

"Aw that's a shame! I think I just saw him go to the *toilets* Sam..."

"Hick...toilets...hick..."

Sam had come over a little queasy with a distinct greenish hue to his face as Mike released him from his one-armed grip. Sam began to make his way to the toilets as the Hen Party went about their business.

"Yeah go find him Sam, he'll help you out!"

Mike watched Sam leave the pub floor passing Will's group who all sniggered at the drunken mess passing them. Mike went back and took the only other seat available at his and Carl's table, Carl had been watching the entire exchange with curiosity as his shag for the evening deposited another fresh drink down; Carl didn't even acknowledge him as he narrowed his eyes at his best friend.

"What did you do Mike?"

"Hmm Carl?"

"What have you done?"

"Nothing my dear friend..."

"*Liza Minnelli lies...*"

Mike chuckled at this and took a swing of his own drink taking his time in the process, and then he responded rather abstractedly.

"38%..."

"I'm sorry, what?"

"38%. That's how much alcohol content is in Sambuca and we all know that can make us say, do or *discover* things we aren't expecting exactly..." Mike used his drink to indicate the still swaying Sam who was just about making it off the pub floor rather slowly in his drunken state. Carl watched surprised as Sam finally disappeared then looked back at his friend raising his drink.

"You clever *Bitch*..."

Billy Harding © 2020

The two deities clinked their glasses together at the toast, smiling devilishly.

Yes, these two had their feet well and truly under the table. Who knew when they would get up and leave it for pastures new in future? Certainly not anytime soon.

Eight

Back In The Pub Toilets.

1:24 AM...

The kissing was firstly, an exploration.

Then it became somewhat reciprocal.

Then it became almost an unsatisfied hunger along with an almost voracious heat to it.

Ryan Tate had ensnared Will in his honey trap and Will was slowly giving in to it, Ryan was for a better expression an eager beaver at the challenge.

His hand was not just on his crotch, it was now on Will's stiff member groping it tightly as it responded to physical touch by throbbing continuously, whilst Will's hands were just starting to fully grope Ryan's pert buttocks clenching them tightly as he got to them, they were not only firm, they were toned which caused a wave of excitement to course through Will's veins in pleasure that he knew he shouldn't be feeling right now but he accepted it in the heated moment. Will was trying to pull away from the embrace, but Ryan was not making it easy at all.

"Fuck Ryan, we have to stop this..."

"Mmmm, Will don't spoil the moment!"

"But...oh bloody hell!"

Ryan was working his way down Will's neck now, then he was going much lower as he used his free hand to start unzipping Will's flies. *'Fuck me I need to stop this'* Will's alarm bells were practically ringing in his mind, but his body was telling him a different story all together. It was responding to Ryan's touch, sex appeal and everything else that came with it. Will hadn't been touched in quite a while before this fateful evening had rolled around so the urges were real thus his body only knew how to react to such temptations, by giving it back just as good. Ryan was now on his knees; Will's flies were fully undone, and Ryan's hand was still massaging the bulge which he kept in Will's briefs for now anyway as Ryan stole a glance looking up at him.

"Well hello there bad boy, can't wait to get at that..."

"Ryan, really please. This shouldn't be happening..."

"Oh, but it really should Will, how badly have you wanted to fuck me anyway!"

"*Grr...*"

Will was losing the will to maintain his already pitiful defence. He knew give or take a few moments he would drag Ryan Tate into the men's toilets singular cubicle and just go for it without a backwards glance, then he heard a noise from just outside like someone was falling over, him and Ryan both looked at the door of the toilets alarmingly then before he knew he had done it he had hoisted Ryan up from the floor with both of his hands and then zipped his flies up in a flash. "Enough of this, we shouldn't have done anything in the first place" Will said as he broke the physical hold of Ryan by taking a big step away as the toilet door almost flew off its hinges to admit Sam Wight who was swaying a lot more than he should have been and he did not look at all well, the greenish quality to his face a big giveaway for one thing. Ryan's eyes widened in shock at the sorry state of his boyfriend, Will just stood there holding his breath, awaiting the metaphorical axe that would be coming to shear his head off clean from his neck if Sam was about to put two and two together.

"Hick...heya boys...hick"

"Sam babe, you don't look so good..."

"Hick...oh me hick, I'm fine...I'm just..."

Sam stopped mid-sentence; he had placed one hand on his stomach whilst the other one was slowly approaching his mouth; his face was a definite violent shade of green now under the harsh fluorescent lighting in the toilets. Ryan grabbed his boyfriend steering him to the singular cubicle. Slamming the door open he practically threw his boyfriend in who saw the toilet seat already up for him, he was on his knees almost too quickly and the sick came up promptly and extremely loudly too. For Will he was never more grateful to fate or karma or whatever higher purpose existed as he placed his hands on his hips, looked up at the florescent light bulb and exhaled slowly. Ryan was rubbing his still throwing up boyfriends back whilst muttering soothing words. Will went to the sink to wash his hands, he felt dirty and very unclean. Looking in the mirror which also needed a good wipe down he saw nothing but shame along with shock plastered on his face staring right back at him in the grubby mirror. Drying his hands, he began to leave the toilets for what he hoped was the last time this eventful night, Ryan was not done with him yet so half blocked his way out having left Sam to still finish throwing up. *'Talk about having no morals'* Will thought grimly *'*.

"Ryan, please stop this, your *boyfriend* needs you!"

"Just one thing I have to say Will Hardley..."

"Fucks sake. Spit it out then?"

Ryan leaned in to kiss him again, but Will turned away, so he only got his cheek this time; he made it a slobbery one as well. Will could now smell the alcohol coming off of him too.

"I will be seeing you later, you can count on that!"

Ryan then returned his attention to his still vomiting boyfriend who was too busy to even notice the sleazy exchange occur or probably even remember if it had happened in the first place. Will was stood there by the open door of the toilets completely numbed from it all, *'you absolute, fucking slag Ryan Tate'* he thought *'I know exactly what this was. This wasn't some way you showing me that you might have liked me, this was you getting a quick horny thrill to add to whatever blacklist you have in your sick mind. And I'm the idiot who more or less went along with it until the reality came literally crashing through the door'* Will marched out of the toilets determined to never enter them again whilst he resided in the pub tonight with the lads for the remainder of their time out. Will was back on the floor of the venue now; he saw the boys chatting away none the wiser to what had just happened to him. Johnny the ever observant one was first in when he saw the look of blatant disgust plastered on Will's face.

"Ok what has happened now Will?"

"I don't wanna talk about it"

"Uh oh Willie boy, you got your knickers in a twist *luv*..."

"Josh, pack it in, *now*."

"Josh don't test Will now babe"

"I was only teasing him Joe..."

"DO YOU KNOW WHAT...?"

Will stopped himself from what he was about to say as his three friends all froze in their places at his sudden outburst. They didn't breathe, move, talk, or even dare to say anything else to tip Will further over his edge of sanity that he was clearly balancing on already. In fact, they were all extremely worried about him.

"Sorry Will, I didn't think I was stepping over the mark..." Josh began.

"Yeah Will babe what's up, we're here..." Joe peace offered.

"We all are" Johnny patted his arm in his signature way, but Will brushed it away casually. Grabbing his still slightly cold Corona Extra he looked all three boys in their eyes, "I'm going outside for a few minutes; don't follow me I want to be left alone. It's nothing to do with you guys, I'm sorry about my outburst..."

And without waiting for a response or acknowledgement, Will took his beer and stormed out of the pub. Johnny, Joe, and Josh all watched him leave.

"Should we go after him?"

"Oh no Johnny, not after that..."

"Yeah give him some space, even I feel bad and I dunno what I've done!"

The three lads all took quick sips of their drinks; all were still curious or in worried states of mind about Will and what any of them could do to help him. For now, they simply did what was asked of them and waited for his return.

*

1:33 AM...

It was quiet outside, there was hardly any smokers accept for two people who each stood in their own spaces enjoying their own personal time. Will stood just on the peripheral of where the pub was situated and the road leading away from it, he was necking back his Corona Extra with aplomb not caring if it would make him sick or just even more numbed after what had happened between him and Ryan. He cared and he didn't want to care at the same time, he simply wanted to block everything out as best he could so alcohol was the only solution helping him in this endeavour. Stopping to take a moment he turned his face to the night sky where there were no stars tonight, only an endless black abyss staring right back at him which did little to alter his mood.

"Someone's hitting the sauce hard tonight aren't they baby..."

Will jumped at the sound of the unexpected but familiar voice behind him. Turning around he saw none other than tonight's act Son of a Tutu sitting on a bench by the side entrance of the pub with a freshly lit cigarette, her stunning headdress still intact and her eyes narrowed mischievously at Will, probing him. "So, come on my *loyal fan.* What's the matter? Tell Aunty Tutu all about it..." the Queen took a generous drag of the cigarette, Will pondered how to start.

"I've been a right slag tonight Tutu..."

"Have you! Was his meat nice?"

"Tutu! It's not a good thing what I am about to tell you."

"Ha! *Honey,* life's not fair but we learn to deal with it dear."

Will couldn't help but give a small laugh at this as the Drag Queen he admired so much smiled wickedly back at him, she indicated the vacant bench next to her and Will graciously took the seat on offer. Sitting down he didn't realise how much he actually needed to take the weight off of his feet, they began aching like background noise you hadn't really noticed before until you stopped for a moment to process how you were feeling, and Will's body was definitely telling him he was fully in the tired zone. Tutu was silent but she never took her eyes off of him, she simply waited patiently for him to be ready until he was. Will looked at her smiling but his eyes; they showed a sadness he rarely ever let people see. It had been one of those nights for sure.

"Tutu my dear Drag Queen. I have done something stupid" Will began.

"With a guy obviously. Unless you're actually straight? Now that would shock me..."

"Well yes there's that and me? Straight? Next thing you'll know about me is every time Christmas comes around, I take up a part-time job working for Santa Claus. Plus, the other stuff..."

"*Other stuff*? There's more to learn than the fact you're a part time elf for Santa?"

"Oh yes. Regardless of the *Santa Claus lie*, I have learned the hard way that I would guess I know where my place truly stands at this establishment all too well tonight."

"Oh, baby I am sorry to hear. And this is to do with whatever happened with this guy as well?"

"You're sorry for me Tutu?"

"Of course! What do you do take me for, some young Queen who thinks she can shady just because she has her war paint on?" Tutu was grinning at Will now who was starting to relax at last. Just being around Tutu was soothing to him.

"My place..." he began again then paused to find the appropriate words, he then found them resuming once more "...well you see I do like it here when I visit and I thought that I was liked by the people here too. I've been visiting this place less frequently lately I know that, but I have been loyal to it regardless. Its place out here in the literal sticks of Essex and the vital purpose it serves to 'the Scene' down here can never and should never be questioned" Will went on as Tutu was listening to him intently only nodding her head occasionally. "Again, I know my visits have been infrequent, but I use to be quite a regular here and I really thought that meant something to these people who live, work and breathe their existences in this rather *shitty town*. That I am come here to show support to local bars out of the way of major cities should show my loyalty to them, right? But the way a *certain* member of staff or how people like say Carl or Mike don't really interact with me just proves they don't really give a shit if I am here tonight or not, I mean the only real reason I am here is to see you perform in all your greatness my dear Drag Queen" Will looked at her which she smiled at approvingly. Will continued with what he needed to get out in the open for his own peace of mind, "to others as well like that guy I know you want to know about, well it looks like I'm nothing but a shiny object he wants to play with and all he wants to do really is get his mouth around my meat while his *boyfriend* is none the wiser to what he is really like. And that's just the kind of people who exist down here. Clearly I shouldn't be making the effort to attend if I get treated like a one-off quickie by one individual while others don't even want to interact with me but only when it suits them when I do come down here right?" Will finished his rant, it felt good to just let it all out in one big hit to someone who he knew he could trust other than the Foursome, well two members of them at least.

The Queen herself didn't respond at first, she took a few more puffs of her cigarette and was looking thoughtfully at the black abyss above them both; the silence on the street was almost comforting too. She then turned to look at her loyal fan with a curious eye in place. "Will this place, it only books me once every few years you see so my ties to the place are also what you could say *a limited capacity*. Hell, I am just grateful for the booking and the chance to crash in one of their guest bedrooms above the place after my second part of my set is done tonight..." Will was hanging off of Tutu's every word at this point "...but baby, listen to Aunty Tutu. Some things never last, things change, *people* change. Or better yet when you keep coming back to a place after a certain amount of time people then show you their real true colours when they don't even suspect their doing it in the first place. And that's when you have to make a decision about not some of it baby, but *all of it*. The whole picture as convoluted as it may be at the moment. That's when you have to take stock of a situation like tonight and ask yourself, is it all really worth the hassle anymore? Or is time to simply move on to something else other than this little place off the beaten path?" Tutu finished letting the questions hang there for Will to absorb. She rubbed Will's arm then gave his shoulder a reassuring squeeze. Will looked away; he had an idea of what to do now as he thought about Tutu's questions, he didn't realise that he had needed. They gave him a clarity he had been sorely lacking but now, now he had something to refocus on.

Billy Harding © 2020

Turning back to the quite literally iconic Drag
Queen he smiled for the first proper time tonight
and it made him feel good inside, well better than
he had with Ryan.

"Thank you, Tutu."

"Your very welcome baby."

Tutu gave him a playful kiss on his forehead then
breathed on it then began to almost shine it like it
was a car bonnet in desperate need of some
attention, Will couldn't help but laugh profusely at
this small gesture which eased him back into
relaxation more, he lived for camaraderie like this
in his life. Once she was finally done messing
about with his forehead and satisfied that Will was
better than he had been before, Tutu arose
statuesque as ever, smoothed down her dress then
adjusted her opulent headdress which was still
secure on top, that thing would never be moving
since it was like a surgical procedure in itself to
put on. Looking back down at her loyal fan in her
tall high heels she gave him one of her approving

nods and started to make her way back into the pub through the side entrance. Before she was fully inside Will called out to her.

"Hey Tutu!"

"Yes baby?"

"You better give us a show back in there."

"Ha! You're gonna love it don't worry about that! If you don't? Well I'll just give some of my friends a call to come sort you out..."

Laughing once more she made it a habit to be dramatic by a camp factor of at least ten and above by strutting back into the pub showing no signs of tiredness despite the late hour it was. *'I don't know she does it but I certainly couldn't do Drag as well as her'* Will amusingly thought.

Looking at his beer he finished it off in quick succession and this time closed his eyes whilst still on the bench enjoying the silence which brought him some peace, the events of what happened with

Ryan earlier felt a like a distant memory that kept getting more and more faint as the time elapsed, Will had to thank Tutu for the help with that. He felt himself starting to drift a little when he heard a small disturbance. Opening his eyes, he turned his head and saw his best friend Johnny standing there ever quiet and all the more introverted but waiting patiently and looking a little nervously at him.

Smirking a little himself Will looked away and let his friend stew for just a bit longer.

"Relax Johnny, I'm actually ok now. You can thank Tutu if you want..."

"Well I was getting worried about you."

"Yes, because we all know how much of a worrier you can be at times..."

"Would you rather I wasn't then?"

Will found himself caught off guard by this sassy comeback from his best mate, turning to face him again Will signalled he could sit at the empty bench with him and Johnny obliged him by doing so.

"So, are you now gonna tell what happened?"

"Mm I guess so..."

"Well something happened when you weren't with us all"

Yeah, I know. It was Ryan Tate..."

Will told Johnny about what happened in the toilets, with all the sordid details included. Johnny just sat there listening, occasionally widening his eyes as the only facial feature of surprise he would give away. Will finished and waited for whatever response would come from his best friend who processed what he had told him.

"Well there is only one thing to say to that..."

"Oh, don't I know and deserve it Johnny"

"It's quite simple really..."

"Just say it, go on."

"Ok then. Ryan Tate is a complete lowest of the low slag's I've ever happened to come across. And he's a bitch too."

"*Yes*, but the same goes for me?"

"Not really..."

"Oh." Will gave a small tut "why is that then?"

"Cause, your my best friend."

Will looked at his friend surprised once more; he was waiting for his friend to put him well in his place, he felt like he had more than deserved it after his shenanigans in the pub toilets. *'Come on bestie you can tell me off. I more than earned it tonight with my behaviour with Ryan. Throw the kitchen sink at me if you want, I'll take it'* Will was thinking desperately at his friend who just sat there looking impassively back at him.

"*What*?" Johnny acted all innocent like it would shield him.

"You can really tell me off Johnny, I can take it."

"There's nothing to tell off Will."

"Well I say there is."

"And I say there isn't."

Both of them widened their eyes in a faceoff at each other, both equally annoying but also doing it to break any tension. They then both smiled at one another. Will kissed his best mate of the cheek in thanks, Johnny just sniggered his approval.

"What have I done to deserve you ah *Johnny Michaels*?"

"I don't know *Will Hardley*."

"You're still a secret slag even if the Joe and Josh don't take my word for it"

"Ok then, if you say so... *"*

Will laughed as he decided to get off the bench from what seemed like a small eternity. His feet were still aching, this time it was much more prominent after all the activity of the night plus his shift at work earlier today.

"Oh boy I need to get into a bed, any bed in fact!" Will stretched out as he suppressed a yawn which Johnny caught then his larynx copied it as he stretched his own head from side to side. "Your lower back giving you some problems now then?" Will asked his mate who nodded his head in response. They were both getting a bit past these late nights out in backwater towns despite only both being twenty-five years old, some people just weren't made for the late-night partying lifestyle. These two boys were prime examples currently. Starting to walk to the front entrance Will was pondering something.

"You know, it's gonna be all the more better if we crash at Josh's tonight then get an early morning train back home from Basildon in the morning, right?"

"Well yeah you are correct but..."

"But? Don't tell me you have a shag waiting up for you here in Southend Johnny?"

His best friend stopped walking and had his signature bug eyed look in his place above his glasses.

"*What now?*"

"Nothing Will, just you being *you*. For you information, I already text Mum before midnight saying I was gonna stay over Josh's tonight after we were done here"

"Ah, you pre-empted then! Clever boy"

"Well one of us has to be and we both know it's not you..."

"*meow Johnny!* There's hope for you yet in the bitchy department after all."

"Well I have learned from the best after all this time..."

The two boys had arrived at the front entrance of the pub chuckling away the double doors awaiting them, Sophie was on the sound system again from behind the bar telling the punters either it was last orders or Tutu was about to begin the last part of her gig as it had been put off for whatever reason to near the end of the night, one way to keep the punters in and the till or card machines ringing happily until the last possible moment. Small independent businesses like this place needed all the help they could get these days now. Johnny made a move to head back inside but stopped short of entering when Will was still standing there looking up at the pub sign silently.

"You ready to come in now Will?"

Johnny indicated the open door and much warmer air-conditioned climate inside, Will shook his head though.

"Ah. Just one more minute outside, I'll be right in I promise. Two more pints of Coke on me ok?"

Johnny gave Will another probing look but kept
any comments to himself like he usually did
anyway. Simply nodding his head Will's best
friend went back inside to join the other two
members of the Foursome. Will retuned his gaze
to the pub sign and continued to stare, lost in his
own thoughts for the moment he had. *'Tutu is
right. After tonight something has got to change
because life changes when you least expect it too.
Yeah sure it's been a memorable one to say the
least but damn I have got to make a decision
before me, and the lads leave here later'* Will
stopped looking at the sign to look in the double
door windows at the crowd. As always, they were
all in the little gatherings keeping to themselves.
The butch lesbians, the two of the group that had
been left to argue amongst themselves out in the
road after they had long been thrown out by
Sophie had given up on their argument to return to
their home or go hit another bar nearby. The Hen
Party were still staggering around but looking like
they were very much on their last legs with no sign
of Ryan or his boyfriend Sam, probably still

chucking his guts up in the toilets which Will
would now be avoiding at all cost. And there were
the two deities Carl and Mike sat atop their gilded
thrones projecting out to all their status or the
status they believed they had, it made Will feel all
the more dismayed at their sorry existence. He saw
his three lads waiting for him inside and smiled at
having them with him tonight despite all the
dramas that had gone on, yet he wouldn't have it
any other way without them. Then Will saw it and
it changed everything in a heartbeat. The cold
realisation crept up his back giving him
Goosebumps to what he had seen earlier, and it
made him feel dreadful again because he was
wondering how it all might unfold for all of the
Foursome later on.

But Will knew something had to be done about it.

Joe was behind Johnny and Josh who had their
backs to him so he was uniquely covered to not be
seen but little did Joe know Will was watching
him looking at his phone at a message from where
was still standing outside and he could not mistake

the colour scheme of the specific app Jo was currently on. All gay guys had probably used the app once in their life at least, especially a Gay Bar like this.

It was the Grindr app.

Joe Mason was responding to a hook-up message no doubt about it. Not for the first time this evening Will's jaw was starting to hit the floor again.

"*Fuck me Joe;* you've got some explaining to do to Josh haven't you..." he muttered to himself out in the cold night air as he prepared to face the music once more as he started to re-enter the pub.

'How the fuck am I gonna sort this one out though!' Will thought alarmingly.

Nothing came to mind and so he went in blind but ready for anything.

Will had a friend's honour to defend.

Nine

The Stage Area.

1:55 AM...

"I will follow him

Follow him wherever he may go

And near him, I always be

For nothing can keep me away

He is my destiny"

Billy Harding © 2020

The crowd were all in different states of drunkenness', euphoria, giddiness, excitement, hysteria, and everything else that came with those happy feelings from this song as Tutu commenced the finale of the second part of her set. For many in the pub that night they were not just avid fans of the classic 1992 hit film *Sister Act,* they all were most certainly die-hard fans. No wonder Tutu had chosen this as her closing number, she had them all enthralled once again, such was her greatness, it was her own specific magical power if you liked. And she wielded it like no one else, using her free hand half like she was her own maestro as the audience reacted at every flourish of her hand, like they were a very amusing and rather disorganized orchestra.

"I will follow him

Ever since he touched my heart, I knew

There isn't an ocean too deep

A mountain so high it can keep

Keep me away

Away from his love"

Half the Foursome was swaying while the other half recorded Tutu on their phones, all were singing along with her as the music picked up a beat entering the chorus. The audience became even more excited all getting into their own grooves or styles of dance that didn't make much sense, even the bar staff were bopping their heads along plus Sophie too as they worked including the DJ who kept an ever-watchful eye on the volume levels.

"I love him!"

"I LOVE HIM" the audience cheered back.

"And where he goes

I'll follow!"

"I'LL FOLLOW!"

The audience repeated like a well-oiled machine despite all of their more than likely higher than usual alcohol content swirling around in their bellies. The Hen Party were the worse off out of everyone in the pub to no one's surprise anymore. The surprise itself probably wore off sometime before or after midnight for all the other patrons. Tutu kept her hold amongst the jubilant crowd.

"There isn't an ocean

Too deep"

"A MOUNTAIN SO HIGH IT CAN KEEP"

"Keep me away

Away from...the Precipice Pub, Southend, THANK YOU!"

Applause started to ripple through the pub for the wondrous Drag Queen as she entered the crescendo with a big finish.

"Away from his...LLLLOOOOVVVVEEEE!"

The applause was now thunderous and seemed to be unending as the music track came to a stop and Tutu lapped up the praise from the well satisfied crowd, the Foursome were also expressing their utter delight.

"Go on Tutu!" Josh clapped enthusiastically for her.

"Yes babes!" Joe was jumping up and down a little on the spot trying to get her attention.

"That's my TUTU up there!" Will was finger pointing a bit over enthusiastically whilst saluting her as well.

"YAAS!" Johnny all of a sudden loudly exclaimed swaying one of his forefingers rapidly in her direction which caught the Drag Queens attention who flashed a smile at him personally followed by an air kiss for good measure. All three of the boys stopped what they were doing, and all looked at Johnny dumbstruck. They were all rooted firmly in place as Johnny kept his finger waving going to

show his appreciation for Tutu. Then he slowly stopped what he was doing when noticed there were three sets of eyes on him. All of a sudden, he dropped his hand smiling bashfully along with raising his eyebrows above his glasses innocently like he always did to deflect unwanted attention.

"*What?*"

He was chuckling nervously now, his introverted ways taking hold once more. The boys were all reverting to some sort of normalcy but still eye balling Johnny.

"Talk about losing yourself Johnny..." Josh noted oddly.

"Yeah babes, you stunned us all" Joe looked at him admiringly.

"I don't know what to even think right now..." Will was perplexed.

Johnny just gave a small tut and folded his arms embarrassed of the limelight he had unexpectedly drawn upon himself. On the stage Tutu was still lapping up her own limelight from the crowd as she shook some of their hands up front in thanks. "Yes, thanks baby...oh no, *thank you*...my pleasure...oh it was *no trouble* at all!" She had now descended from the raised platform that passed as a sort of a stage with great ease despite her towering high heels; she really was a professional at what she did then started to make her way to the bar so she could de-Drag outback and probably collapse into the guest bedroom upstairs the pub were loaning her for the night. The audience were around her showering her with more praise, thanks and asking for a quick selfie or two which she happily obliged. Looking over her shoulder for a moment she saw Will who was waving at her and she mouthed her goodbye to him which he responded her with a heart gesture he made from his hands which got a genuine look of affection from Tutu. *'I really do love everything you do Tutu, you've made this night just that little bit more bearable for me, bless you'* Will approvingly thought as she finally made to the bar relatively unscathed with Sophie awaiting her with an outstretched hand to pry her away from the last of the gaggle of people around her peripheral, ironically it was some errant members of the Hen Party who were almost besides themselves as they stood there in awe of Tutu, clearly far too intoxicated for their own good. Will couldn't help himself but chuckle at the sorry state of the Hen Party who seemed to have splintered away from one another now as they started winding down or more or less collapsing from their night of heavy drinking. The Bride to be seemed to be the only one lasting the distance as she was at the bar trying to persuade one of the staff to give her one last shot of anything alcoholic but they were just shaking their heads collectively in refusal, clearly Sophie had at last cut the Party off. But the Bride was giving it all she got however despite her drunken mannerisms. Will saw she was being watched with mild fascination by Carl and Mike who were both chuckling at her as she was clearly having a somewhat difficult time of trying to hold herself up as she continued her begging act to the

bar staff, *'you cheeky pair of bitches'* Will gave
them both an up and down look unapproved of
their clearly elitist attitude. Feeling sorry for the
Bride to be Will marched over to her in quick
succession, tapped her on the back which she
turned around to and he indicated a stray bar stool
next to her which she gratefully accepted as he
helped her up to sit then she went back to trying to
pry out whatever form of alcohol from the staff
she could whilst Will had returned some dignity to
her. Doing a full one eighty turn to face Carl and
Mike directly he intentionally folded his arms and
Will Hardley plastered the best putdown face on
he could muster despite being beyond shattered
then stared the bitchy duo down for all his worth.
Mike's condescending chuckling scaled back
immediately as he looked away to anything else
that would take his attention in the pub whilst Carl
had stopped laughing all together then met Will's
stare head on. Will however didn't let up then
upped the blatant disgust on his face at Carl by a
good factor of fifty, Carl then simply looked past
one of Will's shoulders to his arranged shag for

the night who came almost trotting over to Carl with his jacket on clearly having finished his shift behind the bar for the night. Carl then looked at Will with a cocked eyebrow almost daring him to do anything then he grabbed the member of staff and planted a generous kiss on his unsuspecting face. When the bar member started to reciprocate the kiss Will just scoffed at the action and returned to the rest of the Foursome with folded arms who were waiting by the pool table for him having missed none of the unspoken drama that had just unfolded before them.

"Well, well Will..." Josh began looking his friend up and down appraisingly.

"What? I was being nice to Bride?"

"I just didn't realise you were a member of the good Samaritans' as a side job that's all?"

"Ha! I'll let you have that one Sullivan since I wasn't expecting that..."

"Well regardless, you did actually do a nice thing for that Bride" Josh noted as he looked at the Bride who had lost the argument with the bar staff and had placed head in one of her hands and seemed to be entering an alcoholic stupor somewhere between sleep or simple incoherence. She seemed comfy on the bar stool Will had supplied, nevertheless. Will was satisfied he had done at least one small good deed tonight, and then he saw them both return to the pub floor. Ryan with his still equally drunk and very much out of it boyfriend. They looked a sorry state as Ryan had obviously tried to support Sam over his shoulder with one of his arms and Ryan simply didn't have the physique or strength to hold him up, so he was half carrying the lad who was clearly none the wiser anymore as to where he was. Some of the Hen Party who had retained some of their own bodily functions half dragged themselves over to help Ryan and they all managed to slump poor deadweight Sam onto the now empty stage vacated by Tutu. Sophie saw Sam now lying on the stage and let the group know immediately he couldn't be left there but was equally more than satisfied when Ryan came over to explain the current situation to her. Will kept himself firmly away and out of reach of Ryan's deadly charms. He noticed he had been staring at what was probably an unhealthy amount of time at Ryan and tore his gaze elsewhere in the pub and saw Mike Harkness staring at him in return who then tried to make it look like again had been doing something else entirely but Will had caught him red-handed in the act. *'Now why the bloody hell was Mike staring at me while I stared at Ryan?'* Will thought as his eyes narrowed as he continued staring some more at Mike was now intentionally getting his coat on and busying himself on his phone with the other hand. *'Now he is trying to not look at me? What the fuck is he playing at...?'* Will may be tired and worn out, but his senses were on alert again as he honed in on Mike like a viper and he did not like this feeling in the pit of his stomach one bit. In fact, he was dreading the likely outcome if he was right. Making himself tear his gaze away at the suspicious Mike Will looked around as the bar was now quieting down, the DJ had lowered the music, the staff members were taking a few last orders under Sophie's watchful eyes and some patrons were simply leaving after the entertainment from Tutu had been completed. It was beginning to feel like a lot more of an empty room now without much of a crowd to occupy its relatively small space. Will looked at the rest of the Foursome who were all on their phones, Josh was checking the time; Johnny was checking social media and Joe. Well Joe was typing away somewhat frantically, Will could only imagine what he was organising once he was done here with the lads and that was another thought that did not entertain Will in the slightest, he didn't have a clue how he could broach the subject without getting Josh inadvertently drawn into the drama, but there was no time like the present. *'Christ, I really don't want one of my friends getting hurt tonight but why do I think they will be either way if I don't do something now...'* he was thinking desperately about what to do, and then the light bulb went off in his mind as if it all made sense now. Will knew what to do.

"Joe?"

"Yes babes?"

"Shall I join you one last cigarette while Johnny and Josh get a final round of soft drinks at the bar for us?"

"Oooo, Will! You're so sweet, great idea as well..."

Will fished out his debit card and waved it at Johnny who was confused as he looked up from his phone. "Johnny do us a favour, get all of us a round of Cokes and get me one last Sambuca shot I am absolutely going to need it" Will drew his best friend in closer then lowered his voice so only they could converse without being noticed. *"Whatever you do, keep Josh with you at your side at all times, I'll literally be a few minutes talking to Joe and I will absolutely need zero disruptions, understand?"* Will was looking Johnny directly in the eyes to make sure he understood he didn't want any interruptions as he pressed his debit card firmly into Johnny's hand.

"Say you understand bestie?"

"O-K sure I understand...is everything ok?"

"Yes, yes. Nothing to worry about. C'mon Joe, *fag time!*"

Will took Joe's hand somewhat forcibly and they were out of the double doors like a shot. *'Here goes nothing'* Will thought as he led Joe to the bench, he had sat at with Tutu earlier, sitting down he took in a sharp breathe bracing himself, then he turned to Joe and went for it.

"Who were you chatting to on Grindr just now then Joe?"

Joe was frozen to the spot, fag in his mouth, lighter at the read but he hadn't yet lit the cigarette. His eyes were alive Will noticed *'let's see what pathetic excuse he is formulating for me'*.

Joe Mason slowly put the lighter down, took the still unlit cigarette out of his mouth placing it back in the box of twenty. He seemed to remember he hadn't breathed for what must have been over a full minute as Will still deadpanned him with his pointed question. Taking a few measured breathes Joe seemed to calm himself then gave a response.

"Oh that? That was just...a friend."

"A friend you say? Shall I translate that for you Joe?"

"Err..." Joe was starting to become rather flustered now with nowhere to go.

"I think I know exactly who this *friend* is. He is someone local to the area that you are going to have a rather *fabulous* time riding his cock into submission if you're into that sort of thing at all after you're done here tonight with me, Johnny, and *Josh*. You remember him, right? The one who gave us a lift here tonight, the one who is our designated driver, the one who most certainly still likes you despite whatever the fuck is going on between you two. The one who after Johnny is a very dear but *close* friend to me and I would hate to see anything happen that would most *definitely* more than upset him if say, I dunno a guy he liked went off to get fucked to kingdom come and back from some fucking stranger off of a *hook-up app*!" he was now back to standing up in a shot breathing quite heavily with anger and looking down at Joe who seemed to be squirming from his place on the bench, surprisingly Joe hadn't look away from Will during all of his statement. He was still breathing laboriously as well.

"C'mon Joe..." Will sat back down slowly "...make me understand why you're doing all of this to Josh?"

"You think I'm doing this on purpose? Having my cake so to speak..."

"You tell me, you're the one hiding your phone. Making sure no one see's what's on it at all. So, trying to have your cake and eat it too seems like more than a reasonable argument wouldn't you say so?"

Joe's shoulders were now slumped in defeat. The jig was up as they say, and he was backed into a corner which Will fully controlled all sides of escape from, the only viable way out was the truth now. The cold hard unflinching truth that nobody would benefit from at all. "Well what can I say, you got me..." Joe let the confession start to fly "yes I have been chatting to a guy on Grindr tonight; yes I am going to his after this to mostly definitely get on top of him and ride that meat for all it's worth and then some which you correctly guessed by the way good *detective skills* there Will. Oh, also I don't just do all the work thank you very much. Whoever this guy is he better do some work or he will be very disappointed when he finds out he can't satisfy me the way *I want*" Joe finished then he resumed to actually have a cigarette this time while Will was once again utterly dumbstruck again at how Joe could speak about something so blasé when there was a fully grown man in the pub right now who liked him for him but it wasn't enough at the moment for Joe, clearly.

'God it's all or nothing with you Joe. I actually can't believe you're this cutthroat. Guess I had to scratch below the surface a bit more than I first thought' the thought sickened Will as much as it kept him focused on what he was trying to do, helping to defend Josh's honour.

"Josh *truly* likes you Joe, why isn't that enough?"

"Because..."

"Because why?"

"*Because* I want it all Will!" Joe snapped at him his eyes flashing whilst maintaining his composure "I want as much attention, flirtations, cock, sex, kissing, *fucking* while I can still have it and *I do* want it in sheer bulk. I am young, fun, tall as fuck plus I know how to sell that to the nth degree. Yes Josh has been and will always be a sweet man who has treated me very well lately but there are still so many *Daddies* out there who are just waiting for me to my hands on their nice thick chests hairy or smooth whatever I don't really care as long as I do my business with them." He took a generous drag of his half-done fag not looking at Will but at the black abyss above them. Will was now at a loss for words; his friends defence in tatters, only one thing remained.

"So that's it then?"

"Pretty much Will."

"Nothing else I can say or do?"

"Nope. One thing however much this may surprise you. I do actually admire your tenacity and bravery however..."

"You admire me?" Will copied "after the amount of bullshit I just called you out on?"

"Yes. Believe it or not Josh has got a damn good friend in you, I mean the sheer nerve it took for you to lure me out here and try and put me in my place or whatever it is you were trying to do? Josh is..."

"Josh is what?"

A new voice then pierced the otherwise quiet night.

Joe didn't stop looking at Will as a truly horrified look swept across his face nearly dropping his finished cigarette at which the voice belonged too. Will hadn't actually noticed anyone else walk up to them either since Joe in all his tallish glory had been blocking the view of the entrance of the pub doors. Turning around slowly to face the new voice was none other than their designated driver, Josh Sullivan himself, with a glass of coke in one hand and holding another one in the other. Both glasses were just slightly shaking despite Josh having a rather impassive face on. His eyes though, they told are far more different story. And it wasn't a good one. Joe then sprung up from the bench; his cuteness factor on with a cheeky grin for added measure, damage control was initiated.

"*Babes*! I didn't hear you sneak up on us, you naughty boy. The things I'm going to do to you later on..."

"Spare me the cock and bull routine Jo. I heard enough of what you had to say to Will just now."

"Oh. You heard some of that then Josh..."

"Oh, I heard exactly what I needed to know plus enough of the sordid details to go along with it."

Will all of a sudden couldn't look at the Joe or Josh as he knew what was about to transpire between them, truthfully, he felt a little bit guilty. Getting up from the bench slowly again he kept his head firmly down looking at the pavement as he began to walk past the boys.

"I'll just leave you two to it then I guess..."

"Yes, Will I think have done *quite enough* for one night wouldn't you say so!" Joe exclaimed as he lit up a fresh cigarette putting on the sulky persona that he was most aggrieved out of all of them present. Josh had placed the two Coke's on the bench table and quickly grabbed Will's arm to stop him leaving; both Joe and Will were equally perplexed by this action. Will looked at Joshes firm hand on his arm then looked up at his friend, Josh wasn't even looking at Will, however. He was in fact looking directly at Joe in the eyes with the still same impassive stare. "Joe. I'm gonna say this only once..." there was a very noticeable amount of steel in Joshes voice now. *'Oh, shit this isn't gonna go well for me either'* Will thought as he readied himself, looking away fearfully.

"Don't you *ever* speak to Will like that in front of me. *Ever again*. Do you understand?"

Will's head snapped round in unadulterated shock.

Josh was now angry, almost so that if the Incredible Hulk himself had decided to partake in a leisurely stroll right there and then in Southend on the opposite side of the road and had happened to have noticed what was going on with the three boys he would have nodded his approval at Josh.

That's how angry Josh was letting both of the boys know he was too. Joe was once again rooted to the spot, unmoving, unblinking, and rightfully shitting his bollocks out. Josh knew he had placed the fear inside him and Will; well he had never been more proud to call Josh Sullivan a friend right now. *'thanks Daddy!'* Will proudly thought as Josh released him slowly from his grip as he still stared Joe down.

"Now apologise to Will immediately Joe then Will, you can go join Johnny back inside."

Joe's mouth hit the proverbial floor while Will smiled at his friend; his *true friend* who just simply folded his arms and stood there waiting patiently. Joe, recovering from his initial shock, opening, and closing his mouth a few times then mustered up some speech into actual words. "Sorry Will" was all he could mutter as he looked down at the ground, utterly shamed as well as being raw and fully exposed for all to bear witness too. Joe Mason had been truly caught in the act; there was no going back to normal now.

"Will, you can head back in now" Josh said as took a somewhat menacing step closer to Joe.

"This won't take long..."

Will Hardley for once in his life didn't question his instructions from his friend; he simply did as he was told, went back inside the pub, smiling all the way as he did so. *'Yeah, fuck you too Joe'.*

*

2:20 AM...

Things had really calmed down in the pub now. Half the crowd were gone; the music was lowered to what was probably its lowest level, Carl Simpson was still intermittently kissing his shag for the night at his and Mike's designated table while Mike seemed to be ordering himself a taxi. The Hen Party were the very last group clumped together as they hovered over the still unconscious Sam who was laying somewhat quite peacefully on the stage while Ryan was still talking to Sophie at the bar his back fully to his poor deluded sap of a boyfriend. Johnny was the other lone figure at the opposite end drinking his Coke and keeping to himself. Will came up and saw the waiting Sambuca shot; he swore that the vicious substance was calling to him like a siren. "Dare I ask how it went outside or do I even want to know what that was even about?" Johnny enquired as he put his half-done drink on the counter; Will noticed that he had developed some dark circles under his eyes that his glasses hid well if you were a casual passerby but not him. "I see someone is more tired than their letting on?" Will noted of his friend as he took a generous gulp of the Coke, he hadn't touched the shot just yet.

"Mm, yep I am. So?"

"So?"

"Outside? You and Joe?"

"Not much to be said now, I did my bit and..."

"Josh took over. I did try and stop him from leaving but...."

"Josh is his own person, yeah I know. Truth be told bestie I am glad Josh turned up when he did, there were...some home truths that he needed to hear shall we say" Will was toying with the shot now, it's clear liquid was still calling to him. Johnny however wasn't as stupid in his tiredness when it came to Will's non-answer; in fact, he just went for the jugular.

"I take this is because Joe was on Grindr messaging a guy, earlier right?"

Will had raised the shot to his mouth then stopped at Johnny's frankness; eyeing his friend up he never took his eyes off him as he finally downed the shot slamming the empty glass on the bar top. Will just looked at his friend silently who did the same back, waiting ever patiently.

'You clever little fucker' Will praised him internally.

A staff member came to retrieve the shot glass then Will stopped them. "One final round of

Sambuca..." he looked at the bar staff deadly serious that obliged the order then turned to look at Johnny again "...for me and my best friend right here, he's more than earned it tonight". Johnny raised his eyebrows in surprise; Will held his hand out for his debit card back which Johnny handed back over still silent then he paid for their last round of alcohol for the night. Handing one to his friend then taking the other one for him Will raised their glasses for a toast.

"To the truth."

Johnny reiterated it as they clinked then they downed the strong liquorice substance in one. After three shots of it tonight Will was at his limit and he knew it. Johnny gave a small cough after taking it then grabbed his Coke to get rid of the strong taste of the deadly shot.

"Good shit right bestie?"

"Yeah it's just strong though. Thanks for that, I'm just going to the toilet..."

"Sure thing, Josh won't be long now I'm sure then we'll be off after whatever has gone down outside with them two."

Johnny nodded that he understood and left to do his business leaving Will alone at the bar. He surveyed the pub in its much quieter setting now, half the lights had been switched off, an old *Kylie Minogue* track was on in the background, the bar staff were cleaning behind the bar top, Sophie was conducting, Carl was now simply eye-fucking his conquest as they held each other, Mike was still on his phone and Ryan Tate was now all of a sudden standing near Will at the bar but not as close as he had been in the toilets earlier, he was for once this eventful evening keeping a respectable distance. *'Bloody hell. He really doesn't give up or he really is more of a stupid horny bitch ruled by his manhood than I care to openly admit'* Will dreaded whatever was about to come next, he really didn't have much strength left anymore. Ryan was looking at his crotch again but hadn't moved from his place at the bar and Will made sure he didn't move either by holding on to the bar harder than he normally would, he didn't trust himself at all in his emotionally drained state. "So, Mr, you had a good night?" Ryan asked casually as he widened his eyes at Will just a fraction letting him silently know what he was still after. Will was not in the mood at all.

"You for real Ryan?"

"Yes, wouldn't ask, would I?"

"*Wow...*"

"Oh Will come on, you loved what I was doing in the toilets earlier, I felt just how big your excitement can actually get you with the right stimulus" Ryan had the audacity to lick his lower lip at this but was somehow keeping his voce lowered and restrained in the same instant, Will was just confused beyond all reason. "So, Will how about it? We could always pick up right where we left off, the Hen's will take care of themselves plus Sam and we could just, you know, go for a *pleasant walk*? Imagine putting that cock of yours inside me at last..." Ryan had taken a risky chance by sidling up to Will just a fraction closer now, daring fate itself to intervene. Will wasn't feeling anything other than mutual disgust at Ryan. *'His boyfriend is out for the count and all he can think about is getting his leg over with me. This guy has zero morals of any kind'* Will's assessment of him was all he needed to not even be slightly tempted by Ryan's offer of a quickie down some alley in Southend, it turned his stomach in knots.

"Well Ryan there is just one thing to say to that..." Will took a step closer.

"Yes Will?" Ryan closed the distance again, not seeming to care who would witness it.

"Well..." Will started stroking Ryan's arm, he quivered just a little at the touch.

"Ryan Tate. I would for starters, gouge my own eyes out with a broken bottle of vodka than ever come within another hundred feet of you and your manipulative cheating ways. I am a twenty five year old gay man who has seen some stuff in his time since coming out at the tender age of sixteen so whatever happened between us tonight in this out of the way, backwater Gay Bar has completely changed the way I think or feel for this place and yes before you attempt to interrupt or dare ask, you are most definitely one of the major factors from my little adventure here this evening..." Will paused with a raised forefinger to take a swig of Coke as Ryan stood there frozen by Will's words, he put the now empty pint glass down to continue, his voice intentionally light with an airy quality to it. "...Now let's get to the *real truth*. You're a good for nothing slut who gets off on cheating on your pathetic lapdog of a boyfriend who may seem like a nice guy but is very easily persuaded because you might as well have pre-conditioned him to be your little bitch of a slave and the fact he can't even see what you really are, well I pity his continued involvement with you *Ryan Tate*. Now I strongly suggest you go back over to your unconscious boyfriend who is definitely going to need you tomorrow morning from his upcoming hangover from hell and you will not look at me, disturb me or even acknowledge me again tonight in this slightly dilapidated place, whatever happened in those toilets between you and me was a monumental mistake that will never, ever happen again, do I make myself clear?" Will smiled sweetly then took a large but conscious step away from Ryan for hopefully this was the last time they would ever converse again. Ryan had a face like a slapped ass. Any form of lustful motive or sexual desire that had existed between the two of them tonight was gone, forever burning in an eternal hellfire somewhere with no chance of resurrection. "Fuck you Will Hardley; it's your loss anyway..." Ryan folded his arms sulkily, but he knew it looked even more pitiful than anything like a concrete defence. Will folded his own arms with a wicked smile still in place, feeling nothing for Ryan anymore but he did narrow his eyes.

"Oh sweetheart. Who are you really without this place to help fester your parasitic existence? Now off you trot, because we're done here, for good." Will then turned his back intentionally to Ryan who silently scoffed, he stood there for a moment staring at Will's back as if it were all a bluff, but he knew in his heart that it wasn't. He had been turned down and properly put in his place. He then walked slowly away with his tail between his legs in defeat back over to the Hen Party who were trying to get his attention anyway. Will had never felt more elated the entire night; it was always good to takedown a person who didn't have the intentions for you other than their own selfish needs. Little had Will known that he had been watched throughout that final exchange by none other than Mike Harkness who was sitting atop his throne silently whilst Carl continued with his conquest. Will saw him looking and didn't like that he was being watched without his consent. *'Two done, one to go, I guess'* he begrudgingly thought as he hauled himself from the bar to head over to Mike, he wanted answers for his shifty looks from earlier. His body was aching now, he needed to just collapse into Joshes car once all of this was over with and try and put everything behind him. "Got your taxi or should I say chariot all sorted Mike?" Will asked uncaringly if it offended him at all, Mike ever the professional laughed it off like it was nothing to. "Ah Will you know how to kid don't ya. Yep the *taxi* is all sorted just waiting it and someone else needs to get himself home with his new friend for the evening..." Mike side-eye his wingman Carl who stopped his heavy petting session with the blonde-haired barman at Mike's little dig.

"For your information Mike I am not going to my home tonight" Carl continued staring at his fancy man as he spoke "my *new friend* here is very nicely putting me up so...", "you can get no sleep tonight Carl?" Will asked which caused Carl to snap his head in Will's direction.

"Do I detect some jealousy there Will?"

"Not even remotely Carl, I'm far too tired for any of that now."

"Aw pity, you don't strike me as a person you can *last the distance* shall we say, no offence intended."

"That's was a good one Carl and no offence taken also..." Will paused as he folded his arms and probed Carl with an inquisitive look "...but that's also not what you said back in May time in *Gran Canaria* however?"

The loaded comment dropped out of the sky like a bomb.

Mike had to cover his mouth as uncontrolled laughter took hold of him, even Carl's shag for the night let out a small snigger looking away. Carl however didn't speak; he simply got up a little bit too quickly flung his jacket on and took his latest notch for the bedpost by the hand to make a quick escape not saying a word, they were at the double doors when Will couldn't help himself with one final comment as a parting gift for Carl.

"I guess we will always that special time then won't we *Carl*!"

He let it out louder than he intended but he didn't regret it for a second, not after tonight. Carl stopped with his latest squeeze who was looking at Carl then at him alarmed at what might happen between them, but Carl was far better at playing the game than that. He looked back vacantly over his shoulder without making any eye contact with Will then he continued out of the pub for the last time that night in a hasty fashion. *'Until next time Carl Simpson'* Will thought smugly as he took the empty seat, he had so very kindly vacated. Mike's was surprised at the confidence of Will despite the late hour, now it was just them two, the staff and the Hen Party left with Johnny still in the toilet.

"And then there were two"

"Yes clearly, what can I do for you Will?"

Will place his hands on the Mike's designated table and simply looked at him for a moment, no words passed between them as Will starred. Mike felt like he was under a microscope all of a sudden as he laughed nervously.

"It was you, wasn't it Mike?"

"What was me?"

"You sent Sam into the toilets earlier because you knew something was going down with me and Ryan, don't deny it. The amount of crappy drama I have endured tonight is more than enough for one person let me tell you that." Will finished with a clearly tired expression, he glanced down at the table as Mike sat opposite with widened eyes. *'Just admit it so I can leave this place Mike, please'* Will was begging internally as he waited for a response.

"Yeah ok, caught me red-handed Will. Sorry."

Mike shrugged as he checked his phone as Will looked in surprise at how easy he had come out with the truth, *'well that was lot less difficult than I thought it would be'*.

You admit it then, just like that?"

"Yeah well there's no point in denying it, your better than that anyway Will..."

"What's that supposed to mean?"

Mike this time let out a tired sigh and then Will looked at him, he looked at him like he was seeing a side of Mike he had never seen before. A side that was getting perhaps a bit too long in the tooth for these sort of shenanigans anymore, it aged him right in front of Will who for the first time this evening felt a little bit sorry for Mike Harkness. *'I guess it is a bit lonely at the top when you work hard for whatever status you carve out in a place like this after all'*. Mike smiled tiredly back at Will then he formed his response.

"What I actually mean is this; you're a nice guy Will. If I didn't like you, I wouldn't invite you things like Gran Canaria Pride like I have done with you, Josh, or Johnny. Yeah sure I know I'm not the best-looking Gay man out there, but I like who I like at the end of the day, even when it comes to this place believe it or not..." he paused to look around the now almost empty pub. Will still didn't understand his behaviour tonight, however. "But you tried to get me found out by Ryan's boyfriend! Yet your claiming you still like me as a person Mike?" he asked the older Gay man who was nodding in agreement. "I know how that looked, you getting found out in a somewhat compromising by someone who is spoken for but that particular person..." He indicated Ryan with the Hen Party were getting ready to leave, their minibus had arrived and was parking up just outside double doors, "well let's just say he needed to be taken down a peg or two. He's been trying to get his foot in the door with the 'Powers That Be' of this place I have given everything too for the better part of this last year and quite frankly, his style is just something that doesn't sit well with me or Carl for that matter." Mike finished with open palms on the table in full view of Will who sat there listening intently, there was one thing still niggling at him just below the surface.

"Why use me like that Mike, why make me the unwilling scapegoat in this entire shitty plan?"

"Because Will..." he got up to leave as he received a text on his phone, his own taxi had arrived as well, "...you Will, really are one of the nicer ones out there in the Gay Community. Yeah sure you make mistakes just like any other Human Being living, breathing, and working on this planet does as well day in, day out. That never stopped you being one of those rare good ones out of a bad bunch now does it though?" Mike let the question hang out there in the void to be left unanswered as he did something unplanned, he calmly walked around his and Carl's designated table they had both made sacrifices for over their dedicated years at the pub, and he entered Will's personal space held his chin softly with his thumb and forefinger looked into Will's blue eyes then placed a very delicate but also light-hearted kiss on Will's lips

Billy Harding © 2020

who reciprocated it in kind. The kiss then lingered just a fraction longer for both of the men to enjoy it a bit more, both were equally aroused. Then Mike stopped it by simply pulling away slowly.

"For what it's worth Will, I really am sorry you had to be used you like that. It won't happen ever again." And just like that, Mike Harkness exited the pub to his awaiting taxi homeward bound without a backwards glance. Will sat there in a haze, *'this night really has become one for the ages'* Will thought as he blinked a few times to focus his tired self, the Hen Party were now exiting the pub as well, the Bride to be was holding up Sam with another one of the Hen's; he seemed to have lost all sense of where he was. *'Poor fucker'* Will felt sorry for him then he saw Ryan carrying their coats and felt instantly less sorry. The Party were all out by the minibus loading themselves onto it in rather different yet uniquely humorous ways which made Will smirk from his vantage point back in the pub. Ryan was the last at what Will now deemed were the infamous double doors, he kept his back to Will but was half in and half out of the pub. He stood there for a moment longer and Will truly thought he might just still have some nerve left in him to sneak a look back at him. But Ryan Tate for the only time that night did the right thing, he didn't look back at Will, he kept on walking with intent and got on the minibus, the driver closed the door then went to his seat to start up the minibus and the Hen Party rolled away as their rather drunken night concluded at the pub as well. Will let out a relieved sigh as it was now him and the bar staff left to their own devices. Johnny then finally returned from the toilets.

"Were you dropping the kids off or something?"

"*What?*"

"Oh, never mind bestie" Will chuckled to himself getting up from the seat.

"You're in a better mood than I left you?" Johnny noted as they both made their way to the double doors. Will looked at his every loyal best friend with a genuine smile. "Yeah well, things change don't they" Will held the door open for Johnny who exited. Will went to join him then stopped himself; he turned back to take one last look at the surroundings.

The bar staff were almost finished cleaning and were beginning to partially restock, the DJ stopped playing whatever camp music track was on and the sound system went silent for the rest of the night, Sophie was now starting to cash the till up.

Another eventful night had ended.

'Goodbye' he thought then he exited the pub for the final time.

Ten

Joshes Car.

2:40 AM...

One half of the Foursome leaned on the back side of the car and simply waited.

Joe and Josh were still talking outside the pub along with a lot of hand gestures from the pair of them. Johnny and Will were far too tired to even attempt to intervene in the soap opera that had wrapped itself around in what was now clearly the point of no return moment for these two former lovers. It was the simple waiting game and it had very much entered its final stages.

"My lower back is hurting" Johnny said as he stretched a little.

"That's nothing, I pretty much stopped feeling both of my feet just gone one o'clock" Will responded by balancing on one foot. Joe and Josh had their voices raised but not close enough to shouting, Josh had now placed both of his hands on Joe's arms like he was pleading with all his might but Joe was casually extracting himself from Joshes pleas taking one hand off of each arm at a time carefully then he was widening the distance between them by stepping back from him, he was making his escape to whatever sexual liaison he had waiting for him down the road.

"Oh dear, this isn't going well is it Will..."

"No shit Sherlock. And we're the ones who are left to pick up the pieces of whatever's been said between those two as per usual" Will rested his face in one of his hands briefly, preparing himself for what would be an interesting car journey home. Johnny stopped leaning on the car boot and walked out into the empty road as they waited for Josh, he folded his arms so he could rub some warmth back into him, the mid-October night was now bitingly cold. "What are we gonna do about Josh? He is probably gonna be more than gutted about this?" Johnny asked as he tried to warm up, Will rolled his eyes then marched over with his still numbed feet and stopped Johnny rubbing his arms only to take over and continued the action for him in a much more vigorous fashion. "Thanks, so any thoughts on what we are gonna do?" the best friend asked again.

"We do what we always do best..."

"Which is?"

"We look after our older friend and give him what he needs..."

Johnny looked at him somewhat blankly; Will looked back at him like it was the most obvious thing in the world.

"We support him..."

Johnny still had his blank stare on.

"We listen to how he feels..."

He stared some more.

"Oh, bloody hell Johnny, we comfort him!"

It all seemed to click into place for him now.

"Oh, I see...do we have too? I mean yeah it's not nice what is happening to them right now, but you know me when it comes to well, *comforting* someone..."

Will looked like his best friend had uttered the most dirtiest and disgraceful thing he had ever heard in his life.

"*What?* You know I'm not one for showing my emotions or thoughts..."

"Or anything for that matter. That doesn't mean you have to come across like a cold-hearted bitch now does it? You'd be coming across no better than most of the lot that walked through those double doors tonight!" Will indicated a thumb back to the pub. Most of the exterior lights had all been switched off now; all save for the light above the pub sign. Johnny bug-eyed his friend for what seemed to be the millionth time that night, he really did think his innocent act could save him every time he pulled that look out. At such a late hour it was really becoming more than tiresome for Will. "Look bestie I'm gonna level with you here" Will took a breather then pressed on "Josh is going to needs us a lot on the journey back to his now. He was really hopeful on working this out with Joe and it's all gone to shit like an unexploded World War Two bomb that's just been unearthed in this god forsaken place." Will stopped placing his hands on his hips, he had put out more than a few personal fires this evening and this particular one that was left was going to require a team effort; he simply didn't have the emotional strength anymore *'just call me the Fairy Gay Father why don't you'*. He looked up at the starless sky for a moment then back to Johnny who still stood there impassively as ever.

"Josh is your friend, too right?"

"Of course, he is Will. He was your friend who you introduced me too then he became mine over time..."

"Then imagine how he is feeling right now over there? He is a gay man in his mid to late thirties which you and I know is more than a death sentence once you hit that thirty bracket save the rare exception for Carl and Mike plus whatever utterly ridiculous set up they have down here. We've only got five more years till the big three-zero ourselves then we're both for the knackers too, so I will repeat myself again cause we all know I repeat myself far too much as it. How do you think Josh is feeling right now over there with that twenty-one-year-old who is about to go get it on with some other *slutty Daddy* tonight...?" Will exhaled slowly, he was spent whilst desperately in need a of a comforting surface to fall asleep on no matter what is was; the back seat of the car look particularly inviting to him at the moment, so he mentally called dibs on it. He went back over to lean back on the car boot waiting for Johnny to respond who had returned to rubbing some warmth back into himself. "If that were me, I think I would be beyond sad..." Johnny began as he re-joined Will to lean, trying to take the pressure off his still aching lower back.

"Beyond sad ah? I'm sure there is a better word out there for that..."

"Ok, I would probably be devastated beyond all reasoning and my self-esteem would be in the gutters..."

"Where would it be then?"

"In Gay Purgatory I think"

"Ha! Funniest thing you've said all night..." Johnny began to give Will the bug-eyed look again but Will was quick to add something on, "...and also probably the most honest thing you could say in relation to them two still over there" Will looked back at the sparring duo. The hand gestures had stopped, and they seemed calmer, but you couldn't miss the distance between them; it was only getting wider as each minute went on. Joe was imminently about to head off for his shag and it looked like Josh had resigned him to the fate. *'Oh, Christ and so it begins'* the dreaded thought almost landed with an almighty thud in Will's mind clear as crystal. "Johnny, get ready for it, he's not gonna be best pleased when he finally comes over" Will prepared himself for the return of Josh while Johnny observed the climax as well. He then side-eyed Will.

"no shit...*Sherlock*" Johnny threw the quote quietly at an unassuming Will who looked proudly back at his friend for making a sassy comeback. "Nice one bestie" Will winked at him then their attention was once more diverted as the noise level spiked to shouting levels. "...yeah well, you're the one

missing out ON ME, DO YOU HEAR ME JOE!"
Josh had now begun yelling somewhat frantically,
Joe had turned around to stomp off up the road
leading away from the pub as Josh watched him
leave. "Don't you even think about ever
messaging me or the boys again Joe Mason, we're
done completely. *ITS OVER*! HOPE HE'S
WORTH IT!" Joshes voice was coming across
almost as hoarse as he still watched Joe leave for
what was the final time, he would probably see
him again. Johnny and Will stood there frozen to
their respective spots not daring to move an inch,
they would wait for Josh to walk over to them, and
this would definitely be a delicate operation.

"Bloody hell Will..."

"I know Johnny; this is not good at all. I've never
seen him that angry before, especially over a
guy..."

"Guess that means Joe has departed all our lives
then..."

"Ooh yes, as the old saying goes, *'another one bites the dust'*"

"That's an iconic *Queen* song..."

"That is entirely appropriate for this situation wouldn't you say so?"

"Yeah. I don't think I'm ready for how Josh is feeling"

"Don't worry bestie..." his friend stole a chance to look at him "...that makes two of us."

Joe was barely visible now having walked down the long road away from the pub, a small pinprick in the distance. Josh was still watching him for as long as he could see him, his shoulders were slumped over, his back faced the boys as they continued to wait by the car; they both didn't have the first clue what to do about comforting their friend. Will then decided to get up and go over to his friend, but a hand stopped him, it was Johnny who didn't look at Will, he was looking at Joshes slumped back.

"Let me do this Will. Someone different for once..."

Will didn't respond, he was amazed by Johnny's risky bravado. Johnny let go of Will and walked slowly over to the still immobile Josh, he took his time but let Josh find out he was waiting just off the edge of his personal space. Josh finally noticed Johnny standing there by moving his head just a fraction to acknowledge him. After everything that just gone down between him and Joe, Josh was surprisingly calm for someone who had more or less cut another wasted opportunity out of his life.

"Guess you two want me to get driving you both back to mine now?"

"That would be nice since it's really cold...you ok?"

"As well as can be..."

"I take it Joe is off to his...*friends* now?" Johnny let the bold but politely worded question hang out in the open for Josh to answer; he got a dirty scoff in return for the suggestion. Johnny took a step closer now that he had engaged with Josh, he touched his arm very lightly and Josh didn't bat it away, but he didn't respond to the small touch either. "What was I thinking ah?" Josh asked but it wasn't necessarily to Johnny, it was for anyone to respond, "You were trying your best with someone who clearly didn't appreciate you. He's the one missing out on you just like you told him so as he chose to walk away from everything you offered, including knowing me and Will" Johnny answered, he had begun to stroke Joshes arm reassuringly now.

"Yeah but at what cost though" Josh glanced down at the pavement in defeat, but very little emotion was escaping his voice. He was much more tougher than he let on.

"I guess the cost might be your sanity?"

"Ha, you think?"

"Well why don't you tell me and Will about it in the car?"

"In a minute I will"

Johnny continued to stroke Joshes arm as he looked up the road one last time for any sign of the departed Joe, there wasn't any, however. It was officially over. Nodding his head in acceptance Josh closed his eyes for a second to collect himself, that's when he got a surprise. Johnny very lightly kissed him on the cheek. Snapping his eyes open he turned his attention towards Johnny with his curiosity peaked.

"What was that for?"

"I felt sorry for you" the arm stroking continued just a fraction faster.

"I don't need your pity Johnny..."

"It's not pity if I feel like you need to be comforted Josh. I just wanted to make you feel better a little...and I don't really know the best way to comfort people. So, I did something which I felt you might like, or was I wrong?"

"Well you certainly *distracted* me I'll give you that..."

"Well I'm glad to help" the arm stroking stopped, and Josh looked down at Johnny's hand still on his arm, it was pleasantly warmed from the friction despite the chilly temperament. Josh looked at Johnny now properly which he allowed him to do. Johnny suited the blue colours he wore tonight, they weren't much of a statement bear in mind but enough to be pleasing to the eyes if you took the time to take notice, navy blue for the top with lighter blue jeans that clung excellently to his long legs and the converses completed the look, Josh even appreciated Johnny's thick rimmed glasses and his styled hair.

"Your quite the geek aren't you Johnny?"

"Well I like my tech stuff yeah; Apple is my dream company to work for"

"Why doesn't that surprise me at all?"

Josh had only just taken notice that he had started slowly stroking Johnny's arm without fully realising it, Johnny began stroking his arm again, it felt nice that they were both doing it without thinking about it. Josh tore his watchful eyes away from Johnny to see if Will was looking and found that he wasn't thankfully, in fact he had gone round to the back door of the car to lean on that so he didn't see what was going on between them, fortunately. "I took the opportunity because I kind of knew Will wouldn't be watching us..." Johnny drew back Joshes attention, "Oh? And why is that?" Josh asked innocently, but had he just added a touch of light-hearted sarcasm in there as well, he couldn't be entirely sure.

"Well, you just had a terrible thing happen to you so me and Will couldn't decide how we were gonna help you out."

"Yeah, I know I can get kind of unrelenting when it comes to basically ending something with someone I like, well *liked*. It's in the past now I guess..."

"It is his loss Josh, don't you ever forget that..." Johnny was being braver now as he closed the gap just a touch more between them which Josh surprisingly liked, "...just remember me and Will are here for..." "*Anything*?" Josh finished the sentence then he laughed softly; he stole a glance by looking into Johnny's eyes directly quickly. Johnny did the same but nothing else happened, not yet anyway. "So, what happens now?" Josh asked Johnny who gave a small shrug, "well I hadn't actually planned on *this* happening, but we could all see it wasn't looking good either way" Johnny answered.

"Was it that obvious the whole night then?"

"Yeah, pretty much, well maybe most of the night or the whole way through though..." another Johnny shrug came Joshes way. Josh shook his head looking at one of the houses rather than Johnny. "Are you ready to end this night here? I

know I certainly am. I need to sleep in a bed..."
Johnny had both of his arms resting just nicely
near Joshes shoulders who entertained it.

"You can share with me tonight Johnny..."

"Really Josh? You're sure?"

"It's that or the sofa?"

"I'll take the bed; Will can have the sofa."

"Will won't be happy about that Johnny..."

"Then let him be like that, me and you..." Johnny
paused for a moment not sure if he should say
what he was really thinking.

"Finish the sentence Johnny."

Josh wasn't asking him, but he was very politely
demanding that he did, he even had his hands now
very loosely around Johnny's lower waist but not
quite on his ass, at least not yet he wanted to be
little bit respectful towards him. Johnny was still
holding back, unsure how he could say what he

was thinking without being insensitive to what had just transpired between him and Joe. He wanted to be as thoughtful as he could since Johnny was simply doing something, he thought that Josh would be greatly appreciative of later when they finally got to his and got in to bed. Johnny decided what to say, he at first released the way they were holding one another so that they weren't physically touching anymore then he held out a singular hand for Josh to take. He did so and their fingers entwined loosely all nice and warmed up from each other's body heat.

"Me and you Josh... Can do *whatever* we like to simply please ourselves after tonight's events, I think we both deserve it or the distraction at least." Johnny stated as a matter of fact then began walking back to the car with Josh trailing behind him; they were both still holding each other's hands loosely. "I think Johnny..." Josh began to say "...that, that is a bloody excellent idea!" which Johnny gave a small laugh that only Josh heard. They both walked back to Joshes car where Will had not witnessed what had occurred between them both; he was still on his phone. As they walked the last little bit of distance towards the vehicle Josh had been openly staring at Johnny's ass in his tight jeans, Johnny saw him doing it and didn't say anything to stop him from doing it, he secretly enjoyed the attention. Will heard their approaching footsteps and got up from leaning by the rear door turning to face them.

"Are we ready boys? Josh mate, you ok?" Will asked still concerned for his friend. "Let's just get in the car ah? We're all freezing our bollocks off in this backwater seaside town which I for one..." Josh unlocked the car and the boys climbed in "...have had more than enough of to last me a small lifetime!" Josh plodded down in the driver's seat, Johnny took the passenger seat at the front and Will practically collapsed into the back, spreading himself out over both chairs and flinging his coat over himself like a blanket shivering a little.

The Foursome had now become the Threesome, one member would never be returning. All three seemed to be ok with this new normal that had come out at the end of this night.

"Josh..."

"Yes Will?"

"I really am sorry about everything that happened with Joe."

"It's ok. Not your fault" Josh had both hands on the steering wheel, but the engine was still off. "I'm sorry too" Johnny said quietly, and Josh patted him on the knee, then his hand lingered there a moment longer than was needed, Johnny didn't move it away. Will however saw it all on show clear as day even if it was the middle of the night. *'Well, well, well'* Will thought *'no rest for the wicked. It really is the quiet ones that slip under the radar isn't it?'* he gleefully noted as he kept quiet in the back not daring to say anything to his friends and their exchange, did they really think he had missed that small action. Who could say but Will decided to keep his mouth shut firmly; for once? "Can we please go back to yours now Josh?" Will asked as he busied himself looking at the content, he had gotten of Tutu tonight on his phone.

"Yeah yeah..." his older friend replied with some finality to his voice "...let's go home."

Josh put the key in the ignition and the car revved into life, Josh didn't set off but he got the car pumped so the heating would kick in to finally warm the boys up. Before he brought the handbrake down to move away Will used the moment to look over his shoulder and out of the rear-view window. The pub was there on its corner, the interior lights had now been switched off including Tutu's guest bedroom upstairs which meant everything must be done for the night, the infamous double doors swung open and the DJ with some of his equipment he could carry by hand exited followed by the last of the bar staff in quick succession, then a few seconds later out

came bar manager Sophie who locked the doors up
then she looked up at the pub sign the only source
of light left on, she crouched down and Will saw a
small box hidden near the double doors, she
opened it, flipped a switch then closed it and
walked off without looking back. Will looked back
up at the sign and the light turned itself off.

 Another night at The Precipice had come and
gone.

"Shall we depart lads?" Josh asked from his seat.

"Yeah I am more than ready" Johnny answered
without looking up from his own phone.

"Let's go Josh, I'm done here too." Will kept
looking at the pub he had experienced so much in
over his many visits.

Josh put the handbrake down and got the car into
first gear set up and slowly pulled away from the
pavement and maintained down the road they were
on, Will watched the pub start to shrink as they
moved away from it. Josh got to the end of the

Billy Harding © 2020

road and used his indicator to turn left where the pub would disappear from view in a few seconds and Will never took his eyes off the place. Josh inspected the road for any approaching traffic and there were none at this late hour. He then turned slowly left and the Precipice simply vanished from Will's view, he closed his eyes tight for just a second, searing the image of the place into his mind so he wouldn't forget it. The good times, the bad times, the many drunken times, and everything else in between, all of the memories, he held onto them tightly. He would never forget them or try not too as best he could. For that small place they had just left served a purpose not just for Will Hardley and his friend's current or former but for so many others who had walked through its doors. It was a safe space to not only protect you but to celebrate all people's identities regardless of their backgrounds or wherever they had come from. A place where you can be yourself if your just discovering who you are or you have had to live your life not exactly as originally planned then The Precipice would be there waiting for you. It always would be. That was the real beauty of such a place like that; forget about all the groups who go there, the people who think they wield power or what they think of you. Be confident in yourself and celebrate who you are, it all starts with acceptance. Will would always be grateful to it for that. And that's why he knew in himself that this would be the last time he was visiting the place. When something had simply reached its natural conclusion in a person's life, he knew it was time to move on from it, so that's exactly what he chose to do as him, Johnny and Josh made their way back through Southend in the car. The roads were silent; most of the houses were dark, their residents asleep and three gay men made their way to their own sleeping arrangement, it was the most peaceful time out of the entire night had been for all of them and Will enjoyed every moment of it. There was just one last thing he had to ask of his best friend, so he did.

"Well then Johnny..." Will began "...let's hear the outcome of your homework assignment." Johnny slowly looked up from his phone, his innocent face fully on as he looked back at Will. "What do you want me to tell you?" his friend asked back, Will shrugged his shoulders as if it was the easiest thing, he could ever ask of him.

"Whatever you would like to tell me and Josh."

"Yeah I wouldn't mind hearing either Johnny..." Josh said from the driving seat as he continued making his way through the streets of the Backwater Town. The clubs were mostly winding down now all accept a couple that probably had late licenses till five am which seemed to be playing their part. Johnny had resorted to looking out of the window like something from the clubs had all of sudden become really interesting, the only interesting thing was some random person being sick outside one of the clubs while one of their friends look at them in despair as the car drove by with the boys, a quick flash of a moment of how their night was unfolding. Will wasn't letting his friend off, not when he had set the assignment for him with the backing of two others that had now become one other, so the majority was still with him.

"Yeah Johnny come on you little geek..." Josh nudged him playfully with his free hand "...spill the beans, pros and cons of that place and don't scrimp on the details since we have a car journey to finish" Josh finished as he put both hands on the steering wheel and slowed the car down just a little, a police car was coming down the road the opposite way on its late night patrol. Johnny gave a tut and folded his arms like he was an aggrieved schoolboy, but he decided to indulge the boys rather than debate it further with them.

"Well tonight was my first time there..."

"We know that" Josh interrupted.

"...and I had no knowledge of what it was like there..."

"Courtesy of a *certain individual* in the backseat here" Will interrupted with a raised hand.

"May I finish please?" Johnny eyeballed Josh and Will who both laughed like the naughty school lads they were acting as. Josh had driven back to the part of Southend where it met the River Thames which was practically invisible due to the lack of stars in the night sky tonight. Johnny searched for the calming waters but gave up promptly as they eluded him as they drove past it now. "We are waiting patiently here *Mr Michaels*" Will said in his most sarcastic voice he could put on. Johnny decided to carry on with his opinion. "Ok, so that place is small and off the beaten track firstly..." Johnny looked at each of the boys satisfied he had their undivided attention, he pressed on. "Secondly, as it was my first time I did noticed that everyone who was there, the Hen Party, the staff, Carl and Mike, *those lesbians...*" he said that almost disdainfully which made Josh and Will both chuckle again, the butch lesbians had deserved to be thrown after they pushed Sophie's buttons a little bit too far after all, the pool table incident was evidence enough. The introverted guy continued with his homework assignment he had been given, "...well all those people, the way they were acting. It was all very *Cliquey* I must say. They all stuck to them like there it was almost a bad thing to even dare to go and talk anyone else in the pub, like their own people would physically disown them on the spot if they even attempted it" Johnny finished by unfolding his arms to relax a bit more. Josh and Will were silent for a moment, but they had questions of their own to ask. "So, what did you make of all their behaviour then Johnny?" Josh asked; they were nearing the A127 dual carriageway now. Johnny looked at the wannabe Daddy he would be sharing a bed with tonight.

"Well it made me feel sad for them"

"You felt actual *sadness* for that lot back there?"

"Well no, not emotional sadness..."

"Oh, you felt *pity* for them!"

"Well yeah. If that's all they do when the go to that place, then what's the point in going there all if the time if you can't meet new people and talk to them? Meeting new people is a part of Life..."

Will hadn't felt the need to interrupt, not yet anyway. Josh was impressed by Johnny as he squeezed his knee again which Will saw. *'Looks like the sofa in the living room is my new bed tonight then whilst these two get down to whatever business upstairs'*. "Got to say you are on to something there Johnny boy, good assessment" Josh praised the introvert who smiled at the compliment. "Right, my turn..." Will clapped his hands together vigorously "would you go back after tonight then?" he asked then waited for the answer. It didn't come at first as Johnny had resumed looking out the passenger window. Impatience driving him Will was trying to get Johnny to respond, "hello there, Earth to Johnny? Anyone home in there?" nothing but more silence. It annoyed Will some more who folded his arms in frustration slumping back in the seats and spreading out. Johnny didn't move or stop looking out from the window, but he decided to respond in the end at his own leisure. "Since that place is out of our way and we can easily see Tutu in London any time we want a lot more than down here..." Johnny Michaels paused for effect, the boys waited patiently for once. "...well the answer is no Will; I wouldn't go back there again" he finished without looking at anyone.

"And that's after just *one visit* to The Precipice as well Josh can you believe it?"

"Yeah, I know Will, says a lot about the kind of place it is right?"

"Oh, hell yeah. I think I have more or less made my mind up about it too..."

"Oh really?"

"Yep, time to leave it behind I think, time for some new adventures elsewhere for this guy."

"What about your best friend?" Johnny asked from the passenger seat, "are you kidding Johnny?

You'll be with me attached at the hip!" Will answered which made Josh laugh.

"Not for the rest of the night Will. Johnny is crashing with me in my bed..."

"I kind of figured that out for myself anyway Josh..."

"Ha, well *first come, first serve!*"

"Yeah, yeah you two enjoy yourselves at my expense why don't ya!"

All three of the boys laughed at this at once and the car drove on to the dual carriageway leaving Southend-On-Sea and its eventful evening far behind. For all their sakes they were all relieved in different ways that was it very much over for them.

It had been quite the night for these three friends, the laughter, the fights, the bitchiness, the alcohol, the Drag performances along with everything else in between. Decisions had been made, experiences had been lived for the first time, a coupling had ended when the warning signs had been more than alarming at the start of the night and then just like Life itself, it ticked along continuing unabated or unending. It did its job while these three friends did theirs too. Life would very much play on under the disco ball inside of The Precipice Pub as well. The music would still be old school camp like always, the drinks would be cheaper than London pricing, a Transsexual would be welcomed with open arms for their uniqueness not their differences, a Lesbian would find her girlfriend when venturing there one night, a Gay man would find his confidence or a conquest depending on his mood for the evening but Life would go on.

It always did.

THE END

A Message from the Novelist

Well dear reader I hope you enjoyed my debut
Novel.

I have to say I am thrilled you got through it to the
end and if you're reading this little message from
yours truly...then you must be really bored right
now!

I truly do hope my little story about a Gay Pub in a
backwater town in Essex was to your liking. I have
personally been playing over and working on the
details and ideas of this story for quite a few years
before I decided to muster up the courage to
finally put this to paper which is what I started
doing in January 2020.

Truth be told I have had a lot of the characters
featured in this story listed down for quite a bit
longer but I was honestly prioritising other story
ideas over this until I thought up the character of

Billy Harding © 2020

Will Hardley and decided that this Novel should be the starting off point for you all to meet him and get to know him a little bit over one evening in an environment he is familiar with. I hope you like him as he will be featured in more upcoming stories in the *Will Hardley Series*.

For now, though please feel free to re-read this story.

If you happen to frequent any Gay Bars or Pubs in the UK or elsewhere in the World and this gives you a little enjoyable nostalgia trip, then this all wasn't for nothing.

It was all worth it.

Thanks for reading once again.

Well that was a night out for Will Hardley & his friends.

Are you wondering when you will see him again?

Have no fear dear reader.

He'll return in *The Workplace…*

Excitement. Nerves. Giddiness. Adrenaline. He felt all of those feelings and more. He could start referring himself as proper staff now that the days of sub-contraction with the *Orbit Group* were officially resigned to the history books for him. *'I just can't believe I am gonna be on £8.00 an hour with a discount card arriving for me in no less than two weeks and no more Sundays for me. Ever!'* that thought made him happiest of all as he arrived on the shop floor at the Ladies Wear Department. He had just finished up the last of his induction training which was near enough a two-day course on the history of the company, where it wanted to go in terms of its ambitions and what it was doing to make itself better financially to last longer in the economic sense. That bit hard been the most boring, Will had been trying extremely hard to fight his eyes that had become a bit heavier than usual at the time, thankfully no one had noticed he had drooped a little while the two female Mentors had prattled on. He had known the two trainers in the time had had been here, he couldn't believe over 2 years of working in the store had gone by for him. When he had done the interview with the lovely duo that consisted of June and Dianne he had been equal parts grateful whilst equals part a little bit on edge, he knew they were a formidable pair when it came to hiring for the company but they were both lovely women with hearts full of love and patience for not only the process but the candidates who they gave each their fair due to sell themselves whomever they might. So, when they had interviewed him, they had treated him the same as anyone else despite his uniform he already wore for the Restaurant at the time. The role-playing exercise done by June was exquisite while Dianne had sat in the corner scoring him, what hadn't been scripted was when all three of them looked at each other and burst out laughing at the predicament they all found themselves in. It was the best unscripted moment in Will's life thus far. He sailed through the rest of the interview process with ease, then he had been offered the job by June and Diane, met the

Manager for the Cafe' for a quick meeting then the rest as they say had been history. He became full time staff with shifts spread across four longer days rather than five since they had tweaked his shifts just a bit so he was taken out of working on Sundays ever again which had floored Will to no end. Their reasoning behind it though more than made sense for them to do it though, all the current staff worked Sundays on either time and a half or double pay due to their old contracts they clung onto. Times were changing in the Retail Sector however and the new company mandate was to cease giving these incentives to work Sunday shifts with those types of pay so they had been phased out over a length of time. One of the things that had been given to Will by pure luck of the draw was the London-weighting, however. The store had been a viable candidate for it for many years since it was located in close proximity to the M25 Motorway but in the last few weeks the store had been chosen to lose its location premium bond as the store when it came down to the technicalities of its actual location was about something over 500 feet outside of the motorway so that was in the midst of being phased out too. Not in Will's case though as he had applied in the time frame, they were in the midst of losing the bond, they had to officially honour giving him London-weighting on his pay, so he was awarded it. He felt like he was the cat who got the cream really. Now here he was, induction completed, and he was on his way down to the Cafe' to do the last few hours of his second day with the company to get his hands truly stuck into the Cafe' way of working. *'I know it's an all women team but I can't wait to work with them, they'll love having a Gay co-worker to bitch with about customers with, that and I love to bitch in general'* the gleeful thought filled him with more happiness as he walked down the escalators. The Cafe's was just off to the side of the Food Department in its own little corner. It was just gone 4 in the afternoon so it wasn't that busy anymore which meant Will would be meeting some of the team today and getting to know them for a bit, he still couldn't wait for it though. He got off the escalator then

walked into the smaller seventy-five seated area,
just as he suspected only about eight or, so tables
were filled at this late hour of the afternoon. All
was calm so he wasn't about to be thrown under
the bus by any surprises thankfully, he took a good
look at the place and was instantly think one thing.
*'This place needs serious refurbishment; I feel like
I've time travelled back to the 90's in a few short
seconds'* he assessed the decor along with the
tables. The floors had probably started as a nice
pleasant cream colour but years and years of
people pummelling them had reduced it to what
could only be described as a pale yellowish hue. It
wasn't pleasant to look at it. He made his way to
the back area of the Cafe' where he knew they all
escaped too from time to time and it was beyond
small, *'how in the world do they all fit in here?'* he
asked himself then it hit him like a tonne of bricks.
It was intentionally designed this way so they all
couldn't fit in here at one time, a shrewd but
effective decision on the manager's part he was
sure of it. Some of the team were out front but
there was no queue or customers to be served, they

were all talking in their own little group, Will observed them and took notice of how physically close they were all standing to each other, it was a strange thing to be doing on the shop floor of all places. *'If this was a busy bar or pub, I would totally get why they are all standing like that, but this is work after all, no need not include anyone else like say, me?'* He was waiting for them to still take notice of him but they hadn't yet in fact he was sure they didn't even know he was standing there waiting patiently to be acknowledged.

"Ahem..." he let out a quiet cough.

The group of women kept on talking none the wiser to the ripple of disturbance.

"*Ahem...*" he made the cough louder now.

One woman with her back to him raised her head at the cough but then resumed her conversation with the group.

'You have got to be kidding me with this right?'
He looked at them all with wide eyes then just
decided to go dive off into the deep end.

"Hello there ladies! I'm Will your new co-worker
from the Restaurant" He chimed in overly loudly
plus a smile to please anyone, half of the group
then jumped while the other half had looks of
annoyance.

"Who was that...?"

"Disturbing our chat, who would dare...?"

"They'd better have a good reason for the
interruption, which was *our time...*"

Will continued smiling as the group of women all
turned to face him at once slowly in an eerily
fashion, each looked at him like he wasn't the new
boy but a new thing, all had a different set of
narrowed eyes, one of them even had some serious
looking teacher-like glasses on. *'Well, this is a bit
of a tough crowd'* He approached them slowly,
none of them made any move to get closer to him,

oh no they were waiting for this new person to come to them. He kept the smiling going even if he felt out of sorts around these women who were now his new co-workers for the foreseeable future. "Hello again ladies, so sorry to interrupt your chat I just wanted to introduce myself again, I'm Will Hardley and I'm going to be working with you all from now on as your new employee" he finished by offering his hand to the one with the serious looking glasses, *'definitely getting a teacher vibe off of you'* Will thought as the group of women all looked at his outstretched hand waiting to shake anyone's hand who would take it. The woman with the glasses stole a quick look off her friends then took Will's still waiting hand, *'whenever you're ready ladies, you can't catch Gay anymore in case any of you are worried about that still...'*

Printed in Great Britain
by Amazon

49067371R00163